Aztlánicon:

Conspiracy of the Senses

by

T. Ervin Wilson

Aztlánicon

Conspiracy of the Senses

KNOW THIS:

Everything within this work of fiction is mere invention of the author's imagination.

Any resemblance to real events or actual persons, living or dead, is either entirely coincidental or the blind luck of a novice.

Names, characters, institutions, systems of magick, treaty agreements, religions, legal fictions or other underworldly entities, are the bitter harvest of the author's imagination, intended as benign false witness, conjured merely to entertain or distract from the chaotic dimension of sentient-human suffering.

Don't say you weren't warned

Author's Note for First Edition

I first became aware of the overshadowing in the fall of 2003. After a long period of lapsed consciousness at the computer, I discovered a number of pages of narrative in the output tray of my printer. I had no idea how they came to be there.

These periods of lapsed consciousness continued for some time and the pages of narrative accumulated until the amount became substantial. I had no rational explanation as to why this process was transpiring through me, but for some irrational reason it seemed important and the pages continued to collect as I maintained an inspired custodial attitude.

At some point, the overshadowing entity made itself known to me by generating a crude title page and a very raw preface. It was made clear that the narrative was to be entitled Aztlánicon. The entity identified itself as '*Sangs.gye rDo.rje*' (Indestructable Buddha). The preface cryptically revealed that *Sangs.gye rDo.rje* was a Tibetan Lama currently between physical incarnations.

Although the source behind the narrative was trancelike and of the nature of the automatic writing, I am justified in claiming authorship of the work because the discarnate *Lama* not only ignored grammar and syntax, but was a piss poor speller. It required every resource at the author's disposal to infuse the work with the flavor of *quantum witness*, the Lama's intended narrator.

The following 'novel' is the residue of this inter-dimensional collaboration.

the author

Author's blog and schedule of telepathic guru yoga

@

http: // stores.lulu.com/t_ervin_wilson

Contents

Codex I

Codex II

Codex III

Codex IV

Codex V

...and all treaties made, or which shall be made, under the authority of the United States, shall be the supreme law of the land; and the judges in every state shall be bound thereby, any thing in the Constitution or laws of any state to the contrary not withstanding.

ARTICLE VI: Section 2
Constitution of the United States

By international law private rights are unaffected by conquest. The conqueror seizes on the possessions of the state, the public property, while private individuals are permitted to retain theirs.

Woodworth v. Fulton
California Supreme Court
Vol. 1, p. 306

Those who speak English or Spanish and are neither English nor Spanish, remain a conquered people.

Sangs.gyes rDo.rje

Quotidian Global Citizen, Inc.

hereafter, extends the blessings and benefits of

Global Corporate Citizenship

to inhabitants of the former nation-states

within the hemisphere known as

the Free Trade Area of the Americas

Quotidian Global Corporate Citizenship

Become a part of the Solution.

The Hope Of the Wicked Is As Dust

1995

Pocoquetzal, Guatemala

40 IT IS NOT TO BE SAID:
THIS IS WORSE THAN THAT:
FOR ALL SHALL BE WELL APPROVED
IN THEIR TIME.

--ECCLESIASTICUS 39

Isadora Caradona lived with her mother and her mother's mother in their ancestral hut on the outskirts of *Pocoquetzal,* a village in Guatemala. The three women were known practitioners of the *magica divina.* The mother's mother was a well regarded *curandera* serving that entire tropic locality. The Caradona women thrived in the natural cycles of the cosmos, their lives were full, even idyllic by third world standards. But, they were also cursed. Each woman, in the course of her spiritual practice, had become witness to her own divinity. It was inevitable that the three would live in a state of primordial sovereignty. Of course, no one is ever rewarded for that.

In 1994, during the Uruguay Round of the GATT, the humanity of an entire hemisphere was subjected to the *gringo's* treaty, known as GATS and it's vile, demonic progeny the

World Takeover Organization.

Within months of the WTO launch, the water of Guatemala fell under the control of Quotidian Global, a ruthless velociraptor of a corporation that was first to take advantage of the revenue opportunities made possible by the treaty. In the wake of the takeover the cost of electricity tripled and the villages of Guatemala were suddenly informed that they needed a license for the water they drew into their reservoirs. In *Pocoquetzal,* the news was not well received by the Village Elders.

The village pre-dated the European conquests and water had been taken from the river for several hundred years. Who were these *gringos* to come in and make the poor village pay for their own water? The Elders stomped and grumbled but eventually conceded and a way was found to comply with the *gringo* extortion.

Eventually, the Quotidian agents found their way to the hut of the Caradona women and demanded that they purchase the license for the water from their well.

"That 's ridiculous. My mother's mother dug that well with her worthless husband fifty years ago." said Isadora.

"You can keep the well. You just can't take our water from it." said the agent.

"When did it become your water?"

"You people are going to have to learn that it's a new era here in Guatemala. If you don't like it go to Cuba."

The well was capped, the expedition vacated, all with the understanding that the well was to stay capped until the Caradona women complied with the water license.

After the Quotidiots left, Isadora sought help from a distant neighbor who uncapped the well. From then on the Caradona women lived low key while sneaking water from their own well. When the Quotidian agent finally returned, his crew re-capped the well. Isadora began walking to get her neighbor before the work was even finished. The agent and his crew were gone when Isadora returned with the neighbor. The cycle began all over.

Aztlánicon
The Hope Of the Wicked Is As Dust

After several similar exchanges the Quotidian Global agent stayed away for a long time. Isadora began to believe that she had outdone the Quotidiots until her mother's mother fell gravely ill. And then her mother. Neither woman responded to treatment. Neither seemed to benefit from prayers to the *orishas*. Isadora lost them both in the same week.

Suddenly alone in the world, Isadora languished in the ancestral hut doing the best she could to survive the increasingly hostile environment created by Quotidian Global. She was forced to carry water from the unpoisoned well of a distant neighbor who could afford the license and was generous enough to allow her access. She could only carry enough water for drinking and cooking. Two or three times a week, she toted pots from the river, where she also bathed. Isadora's life had turned into a lonely, primitive struggle to survive.

On one such trip from the river, Isadora struggled with two large pots of water and had almost made it back to the hut when she became unconscious and collapsed to the ground.

∴ Ω ∴

Isadora had no idea she was in a coma, but really whoever does? She became aware that she stood under some trees alongside a small lake. Tranquil herons waded through the shallow misted water along the banks. Otherwise, it was in a rather unremarkable scene she found herself. Unremarkable until she began to perceive a tiny voice.

"Come and find me, *m'hija*."

Although the voice had no locality, Isadora was drawn toward the mist gathering off the lake. High in the trees was a glow that modulated with the tiny voice, so faintly, it could scarcely be heard.

"You must come and find me, *m'hija*."

Isadora had no rational reason for knowing that this was the voice of the *Virgen*, but she knew it just the same.

"Where do I find you? "

"In *Aztlán*, by the little lake named Painted Pony."

Isadora mulled over what was being said to her.

"*Aztlán* is too far. How will I get there?"

"That will work out."

"If I do get there,.... then what?"

"Then you will be my messenger."

"Messenger of what?"

"You ask many questions for someone in dire circumstances." As the voice said those words, the glow in the mist intensified.

Then the context of the dream changed. Suddenly, there was the music of *mariachis*. the unremarkable area was now crowded with people. Isadora found herself hoisted upon a chair by several men shouting *viva*. Around them were women cloaked in reverence, they reached out at Isadora to be touched by her. The men carried Isadora next to a signpost in the ground. They held the chair up high to where Isadora could see that the sign was blank, but still the chair raised and lowered to the shouts of '*viva*'.

The voice again spoke to Isadora as the shouts continued," Deliver my message to the people, *m'hija*, *La tierra promesa est aqui y ahora.*"

In her hand, Isadora discovered a writing instrument capable of functioning in such a dream. She reached out to write the *Virgen*'s message on the sign, but the celebration was too robust, the devotion too needy.

Aztlánicon
The Hope Of the Wicked Is As Dust

Regretably, it was impossible to write down the *Virgen*'s message in this particular dream. As the mindstream known as Isadora slowly drifted back into the potent, infinite darkness, she was already craving the lost adoration.

∴ Ω ∴

Isadora was lying on familiar jungled earth when she regained waking consciousness. The energy was fresh, with vivid traces of the mission given to her by the *Virgen*. Again, there was the possibility of meaning in her existence. Since the *gringos* had invaded her life, perhaps it was time to invade theirs. Almost everything was sold and Isadora was shocked to find it brought almost nothing. All she took were some clothes and a barely portable apparatus her mother's mother had constructed for the practice of *magica divina*.

∴ Ω ∴

It was widely known that to slip north was difficult and dangerous without the services of *coyotes*. It was dangerous even with the services of *coyotes*. Isadora asked around about passage to Aztlán, but found that her finances were too depleted. Her journey had stalled in Veracruz, where she loitered for months, enduring the indignities a woman away from home suffers in order to survive. During one back alley encounter, Isadora became momentarily familiar with an agent of *la tuberias*, the *coyote* operation of *la familia Salamanca*.

"You're from Aztlán, right?"said Isadora from her knees, as she reached into his pants.

"Yes."

"Ever heard of a lake called Painted Pony?"

"Of course, it goes right up to *La casa de Salamanca*."

"Would you take me there?"

"Why would you want to go there?"

" I have to go there. I have to find someone."

"Who?"

"I can't tell you that."

"For someone that needs help you're very uncooperative. Give me something I can go to my *Doña* with and convince her to let you make the trip on deferred payment."

"You can do that?"

"Sometimes. If the reasons are good enough. If she has reason to trust you won't skip out on your payments and make us come looking for you."

"No, I've heard about what happens to those they have to come looking for."

"As long as we understand each other. I still don't know why getting to that little lake is so important ."

"It's a mission given to me by the *Virgen*."

"What kind of mission could the *Virgen* give to a little *alambrista* like you?"

"She sent me to find something."

"I sent you to find something in my trousers. Let's finish that mission before we discuss taking you to *Aztlán*."

In the aftermath of Isadora's performance of her side of the verbal contract, the agent from *la tuberius* did indeed convey to his *Doña* about the sickly *chica* from Guatemala who was on a mission given to her by the

Virgen de Guadalupe.

$$\therefore \Omega \therefore$$

The clandestine vehicles would always arrive in the dead of night from different directions. The migrants would be extracted from the hidden compartments that were cleverly adapted to each vehicle. There was a panel truck, a bobtail, an RV and a German touring bus with sleeping births. If the bus might be stopped, the driver would hold up a bunch of phony passports and claim that the bus was filled with German tourists under the influence of a distant time zone and thus asleep, under 'heavy jet-lag'. It worked very well and required serious payment from those that made the journey.

Following their extraction, the migrants were huddled together under dim lights and told that *Doña* Salamanca had arranged for them to eat a good meal and each of them would be provided with a temporary place to sleep. The following morning they would actually meet with her. For any migrant fortunate enough to deal with *la tuberias*, *Doña* Salamanca was usually the first friendly face of the often demoralizing journey.

When *Don* Emiliano was still alive, Rosalie Salamanca oversaw the settlement of the migrants into jobs and housing and when those were accomplished she spread the gospel of revolution and *Aztlán*. To these humble people who had traveled so far, she was their fountainhead of survival during their hidden stay in the promised land.

In the crisp morning light, the *Doña* would wander among them as they gathered in the compound eating whatever Carmella Iroñia had arranged for their breakfast. Always accompanied by her scribe, the *Doña* would give notes about the various migrants and where to assign them. Although the *Doña* could apprehend their energy, the weak impressions given off by most of them revealed little and the *Doña* usually resorted to asking them questions to gain some measure of them. When she'd interviewed them all, she would address them collectively.

"Welcome to Aztlán. From this moment on you are each soldiers in the reconquest of Aztlán. *Viva la revolucion!*"

"*Viva la revolucion!*" returned the little crowd with various degrees of enthusiasm.

"Any questions?"

"Yes, mam, how do we help the *revolucion*?" said one mangy *perro* who would surely end up a field hand.

The *Doña* looked at him to see if he was being a smartass.

"There are four things you can do to help the *revolucion*. One, just being here helps. Being here and using up the *gringo's* resources. By any means necessary. Two, you help the *revolucion* by doing what you are told to do. We can't conduct an effective battleplan if everyone is off doing their own thing. Is everyone with me so far?"

The crowd nodded in agreement, waiting for her to continue.

"Three. Most important,... continue to make your deferred payments. We can't conduct our *revolucion* without money."

The migrants looked around at the lavish grounds and the magnificent *hacienda* and tried to imagine exactly how much of the *coyote* fees were left to fund the *revolucion*.

"*Doña*, you said there were four things." said the mangy *perro*.

Aztlánicon

"The fourth way to help the *revolucion* is to not make us have to come looking for you."

Some of the migrants wanted to think she was kidding, there were even a couple of snickers. The *Doña* wanted them to know she wasn't .

"If there ever comes a time when you want to desert the tasks you are given, ask yourself if it's worth trading the role of *reconquistador* for hunted refugee."

At that point Isadora Caradona mustered her courage and timidly put up her hand. Unrecognized, she inched forward until the *Doña* eventually noticed her.

"Yes, do you have a question?"

"*Si, Doña.* Please mam, where is Painted Pony Lake from here?"

There were several snickers among the crowd.

"It's right behind you, over there. Turn around and walk straight for two hundred meters and you'll drown in it."

As everyone took the moment to feel superior at the *indio's* expense, *Doña* Salamanca leaned over to Carmella.

"Keep your eye on that one. I don't know what it is yet, but, there's something about her that's special."

Almost immediately a rivalry was born. Carmella Iroñia had been at the *Doña's* side for many years, so many years that she'd become invisible. It was painful for her to watch this *indio* show up from nowhere and get the *Doña's* notice. This was beyond unfair and Carmella resolved not to stand for it.

.∴ Ω ∴.

Because the *Doña* thought Isadora Caradona appeared sickly, she was assigned to work around the *hacienda*. That way Carmella could keep an eye on her, as instructed. Most days were aggrevating for Carmella as Isadora would disappear for hours. The aggrevation was not from the shirking of a responsibility or anything like that because Isadora usually worked into the night to complete the tasks assigned to her, Carmella had simply had enough of her disappearing in the middle of the day, everyday.

"Isadora, come here. What are you up to?" said Carmella.

"Mam?"

"Where do you vanish to everyday about this time?"

"I'm not sure I should tell you, mam."

"You'll tell me or I'll have you sent back to Guatemala."

"Oh, please don't do that."

"Then tell me where you go everyday."

"I walk to the other side of the lake to visit the *Virgen*."

"What are you talking about? I've spent many days in that park, there's no *Virgen* over there."

"Oh, but there is."

"Very well. If you're going to lie about it. I guess I'll have to report this to the *Doña*."

"I may as well take you to her. She wants me to spread her message anyway."

Aztlánicon
The Hope Of the Wicked Is As Dust

Carmella Iroñia accompanied Isadora on the widdershim pathway around Painted Pony Lake until they came to a grove of *encina* oaks, just like the coma/dream.

"So where is this *Virgen*?"

"She's up there in the tree."

"I don't see anything. Just a tree."

"She's up there."

"This is ridiculous." said Carmella Iroñia as she turned and walked in the deocil direction toward *la Casa Salamanca*. When the foliage got thick and she couldn't be seen, Carmella squatted in the bushes, careful not to fall into the water and watched from a distance, as Isadora obviously thought no one was watching. Isadora walked over to some bushes and pulled out a strange wooden box. From the effort she expended, it seemed the box was heavy. Isadora set the box at the foot of one of the *encinas* and prostrated herself. Her hands formed the *atmanjali mudra* and she prayed. After a long moment she pulled an apparatus from the box. The apparatus seemed spiritual in orientation and involved mirrors and copper and shards of crystal. Isadora aligned the apparatus so that sunlight reflected somewhere into the tree. Carmella couldn't tell where .

Isadora got the sunlight focussed on one particular spot on one particular tree. She sat upon the wooden box and took in each hand the ends of the cables that extended from the spiritual apparatus. Isadora's head tilted slightly upward and then suddenly jolted back with great force, like she was being electrocuted. Isadora let go of the apparatus and collapsed to the ground.

"This is how she spends her afternoons?" said Carmella Iroñia, who was both terrified and captivated at that same moment. The power involved in what she'd just witnessed was humbling, but, Carmella wanted to see where all of this led and simply left Isadora to her fate.

∴ Ω ∴

After several weeks, Isadora Caradona no longer appeared sickly and the *Doña* wanted to know why. Carmella told everyone that she was called into the *hacienda.* It was really the courtyard, which was even better. Carmella coveted any time she could spend in the *Doña's* courtyard. She loved it's lush foliage and the way that it resonated with the sacred energy of the *revolucion.*

When Carmella presented herself, the *Doña* was overseeing additions to the panoramic murals that dominated the courtyard wallspace. Carmella stood in the center and slowly turned to take in each mural fully. There was the 'Delegate in wrestler mask at the *Chicano Congresso de Aztlan"* painted as Diego Rivera would have done it. Next to that was the "*Alcachofa* Field Executions"with the brushstrokes and audacity of Orozco.

Carmella's captivation abruptly ended with the approach of *Doña* Salamanca.

"I hope that I'm not taking you away from your duties. Tell me about what is going on with this Guatemalan *chica*?"

"*Domina?*"

"I told you to keep an eye on her. Have you?"

"Yes, Mam."

"Then give me a report. She seemed at death's door when she got here. Now, she enjoys radiant health all of a sudden."

"Something in *Aztlán* obviously agrees with her."

"Yes. And I want to know what it is."

"Domina, It's not my fault. She's hard to keep track of. She disappears for several hours each day."

"Is she behind on her work?"

"No, mam."

"Where does she disappear to?"

"I don't know."

"Honestly, Carmella you're slipping. Maybe I should replace you with this Guatemalan *chica*. At least, she sounds on the way up. She does her work and still makes time for something extra."

A chill shivered through Carmella Iroñia at hearing those words.

"Find out why her health is so much better. Or else, perhaps I will replace you. You can go back to your duties, for the time being."

The *Doña* turned and walked away.

∴ ☊ ∴

When Carmella came upon the *encina* grove, Isadora was already on the ground, unconscious. Carmella took the opportunity to see what was with this tree. She looked up to where the sunbeam was shining and God-damn if it didn't look like the *Virgen de Guadalupe* glancing down at her. At the foot of the tree was a small sign which said *'La tierra promesa est aqui y ahora'*.

Carmella went over and gently tried to bring Isadora back to consciousness.

"Isadora. Wake up."

Isadora stirred and eventually came around.

"What is it? Is something wrong?" she said, still on the ground.

"What is it you do with this?" said Carmella, pointing at the apparatus.

"I reflect the sunbeams onto the *Virgen* and connect with her energy."

"Do you need it to connect with the *Virgen*?"

"No, I suppose not. You could probably just use a mirror. It wouldn't be as strong as the energy given off by the magick device."

"Where did this come from?"

"My Mother's Mother made it."

"But if you had to chose one as more important, would it be the device or the tree."

"Absolutely the tree."

"What about this little sign over here?"

"That's the message the *Virgen* gave me to spread among the people of *Aztlán*."

Carmella looked around and saw that no one was in sight. She turned to Isadora.

"You don't need to worry, I will spread the *Virgen's* message for you."

"What?" said Isadora.

Carmella pulled a hammer out from her barn coat and pounced upon Isadora, striking her twice in the skull as hard as she could. Isadora was instantly lifeless.

Aztlánicon
The Hope Of the Wicked Is As Dust

Carmella dragged the slight corpse out onto the fishing pier and then went back to get the apparatus. She tied the copper wires around the corpse's neck and then broke one of the mirrors off. She closed the box and pushed the whole mess into the lake, watching the blessed pilgrim sink into the cold darkness.

$$\therefore \Omega \therefore$$

It was a bright, crisp morning as *Doña* Salamanca made her way through the new batch of *peregrinos*. She bestowed her inspiring words on the vital contribution the migrants make to the *revolucion* and she conducted the brief interviews to determine where each new *aztláno* warrior would be dispatched. Before she left for the morning, the *Doña* approached Carmella Iroñia.

"So what do you have to report?"

"*Domina*, I think we're going to have to go looking for her. She's disappeared."

"I thought she was doing so well."

"Perhaps the improvement in her health caused her to run off with some man."

"Did you ever find out what accounted for the improvement in her health? Or, where she was disappearing to?"

"No, *domina*."

"Very well, keep me informed if she turns up."

"I will, *domina*."

As Carmella watched the *Doña* walk toward the *hacienda* she knew that she would only need to endure her lowly position for a short while longer. Thanks to the *indio's* sacrifice, she would soon be known as Carmella Iroñia, the revealer of *milagros;* and not only would her station in life improve, but the people of *Aztlán* would have their icon. This truly was the promised land.

This truly was the promised land.

That Ye May Be The Children Of Light

1998
Waltonville, Aztlán

15 UNTO THE PURE ALL THINGS ARE PURE:
BUT UNTO THEM THAT ARE DEFILED AND UNBELIEVING
IS NOTHING PURE;
--PAUL'S FIRST EPISTLE TO TITUS

In the spring of that twenty-sixth year of the hidden revolution, by metaphysical exertion unknown to the average fleshbound human, the miraculous image of the *Virgen de Guadalupe*, Holy Saint of the *Americas,* revealed herself to Carmella Ironía, not on the side of a glass building, nor on the face of a grilled cheese sandwich, as the fleshbound had come to expect, but high off the ground in the bark of an *encina* oak on the banks of Painted Pony Lake.

The *place of miracles* was set apart from the rest of the county park that bordered Painted Pony Lake. The *milagro* stood at the bottom of a path thought treacherous by some, a path that few would choose to tread if there wasn't a *milagro* below. At the foot of the challenging path was an area cordoned off by a thick wire fence dressed with flowers and ziplock bags that contained pictures of loved ones and prayers to the *Virgen*. Within the fence, the area was taken up with strange, confusing benches that undulated upon tumultuous ground, bulged by roots and rutted by runoff from the adjacent hillside. At the foot of the sacred tree were two large candle stands constructed of unadorned sheet metal to protect the many votives from the winds and rains, which some years came often.

Aztlánicon
CODEX I

On the perimeter of this awkward ground stood a bilingual sign which offered the only account of what had gone on here.

THIS IS A PLACE OF PILGRIMAGE AND PRAYER.

IT IS REPORTED THAT THE VIRGIN MARY
APPEARED HERE ON JUNE 17, 1994
TO CARMELLA IROÑIA,
A PILGRIM SEEKING DIVINE HELP.

SOME SEE AN IMAGE OF THE VIRGIN OF GUADALUPE
ON THE TREE OPPOSITE YOU.

ESTE ES LUGAR DE PEREGRINOS Y ORACIÓN

SE HA REPORTADO QUE LA VIRGEN MARIA
APARCIÓ AQUI EL 17 DE JUIO DE 1994
A CARMELLA IROÑIA
UNA PEREGRINA BUSCABA AYUDA DIVINA.

ALGUNOS MIRAN UNA IMAGEN DE LA VIRGEN DE GUADALUPE
EN EL ÁRBOL QUE ESTÁ ATRÁS DE USTED.

La tierra promesa est aqui y ahora.

Like almost anything official in modern Aztlán, this sign was bullshit in two languages. None of the local *Aztlános* had any faith that the Virgin Mary was involved in any of this. Anyone who knew of the Carmella rumors, knew it was the *Virgen de Guadalupe* who came to her in a vision and gave her the 'message to *la raza*' .

The posting of the bilingual sign was a bitter, contentious affair between the *aztlanos* and the city fathers. There was an enormous outcry against the Virgin Mary. Among some of the *aztlános*, the Virgin Mary was a symbol of religious colonialism. The only thing on which anyone in power could agree was that there were too many virgins for anyone's good. As expected, the city fathers decided to downplay the brown one and offered the 'Guadalupe compromise', which was merely to add a sentence acknowledging that some believed they saw the *Virgen de Guadalupe* in the tree.

∴ Ω ∴

Rumors spread throughout the secret land that the *Virgen de Guadalupe* had not only healed Carmella Iroñia of some grave, unspecified affliction, but the Saint had also miraculously left her image in the bark of a tree. The rumors stirred the entire region. Not a soul in Waltonville could remember anything that attracted so many *gringos* down to the park that surrounded Painted Pony Lake. Most *gringos* never even ventured down to the bottom third of the county, which was just fine with the *aztlános*.

Once satisfied that the rumors were true that the *espiritu santa* did truly dwell in this lagoon of miracles, Lucha Obregon began to bring her great grandchild, *Jesus,* as often as possible. Many local women did the same with their male children, all with the fervent hope that the divine energy of the place would somehow influence them away from *la vida loca.* It rarely manifested like that. Lucha was certain that it must somehow please the Gods on high to witness the endless parade of male folly.

Despite Lucha's fondness for *Jesus,* she retained a hurtful detachment toward the child and never for a second considered initiating him into the matrilineage of *magica divina.* She had no faith that he might have capacity. After all, in Lucha's life, males had proved themselves to be portals of misery rather than benefit; useful only for heavy labor, slaughtering each other, and, of course, the delivery of spermatazoa.

∴ Ω ∴

As Lucha sat with the stroller within the *milagro* area, motion stirred in her sense field, she looked up to see a woman bearing a wry grin and something in her hands. Lucha had seen this woman before. She was usually seated at a small card table near the fishing pier, available to pilgrims for tarot readings. Lucha grabbed the stroller firmly and braced for any number of bad things that could happen. What did this stranger possibly want? To discourage the gypsy woman's approach, Lucha summoned the *energia* and envisioned a huge radiant boundary around herself and the child.

The woman stopped abruptly, with her eyelids partially opened like a *chihuahua* getting it's belly rubbed, she obviously felt the energy. The woman opened her eyes and looked at Lucha with a sense of admiration. She then giggled as she waved her left hand in an outward arc, displacing the boundary and continued her approach.

"I'm sorry. I realize that you were banishing me, but I just had to meet you."

Lucha was shocked that this person not only sensed the energetic shield, she seemed to know where it was coming from. Whoever this was, Lucha knew that she was sensitive. The woman offered something in her hand.

"What's this?" said Lucha.

"It's a mirror."

"I can see it's a mirror. Why are you giving it to me?"

"People like to use them to reflect sunbeams onto the *Virgen*. It's a way of connecting with her."

"I've seen people do that here. But, why are you giving this to me? You don't even know me."

"It makes more sense if you look at the back of it."

Lucha glanced down at the obverse side of the mirror,

on it was printed:

Carmella Ironía
Spiritual Advisor
Receiver of and Witness to Miracles
(831) 999-9991

"You've made it into a business card. Very clever. Carmella Iroñia. Thee Carmella Iroñia?" said Lucha as she pointed toward the bilingual sign.

"The very same. What's your name?"

Lucha extended her hand, " I'm Lucha, Lucha Obregon."

Carmella looked down at the child in the *gringo* stroller, "How many does this make? You seem too old to have a child this young."

"He's not mine. He's my great-grandson."

"Oh, now all of a sudden, you seem too young to be a great grandmother." said Carmella with a laugh.

"Well, which is it? Too old or too young?"

"I'm sorry. I've butted in and stepped into a pile of it. I do that once in a while. I'm a bit of a gossip."

"Don't worry about it, you meant no harm. Did you?"

"No. I most certainly did not." said Carmella. "I really came over here because you seem troubled and I wondered if I could be of help."

"We live near here and I come because it's peaceful and the boy likes it ." said Lucha, as she stopped and thought about what she was saying. "No. I guess I came here because I am a little down."

"You come here for the *Virgen*." said Carmella.

"Yes,... I bring him here to see the *Virgen*."

"You don't come to see her?"

"I don't have to come here to see the *Virgen Guadalupe*. She's everywhere, everywhere she wants to be and a few places she doesn't. She's not confined to this park."

"I knew it. You're a practitioner, aren't you?"

"What do you mean by that?"

"You practice the *magica divina* don't you?"

Lucha was startled, "Look, that's not a question to be asking someone you don't even know."

"I'll take that as a yes." said Carmella. "What you're saying about the *Virgen* is what I believe also, but, I can't afford to look at it that way, you know business and all."

"That's right, as a spiritual advisor, you depend upon people not being in touch with spirit. That's your job,... right?"

"Everyone's got to do something. Why? Do you think I cheat people?" said Carmella,

"How would I know that?"

"Don't you believe it's possible to act as a spiritual go-between?"

"Whatever can be conceived, can exist, is what I believe."

"See? We do have common ground." said Carmella as she reached into her bag and pulled out a pouch, she reached into the pouch and held up a deck of cards.

"Let me do a reading for you,... on the house." said Carmella.

"Why would you want to give a complete stranger a free reading?"

"For some reason you fascinate me."

Lucha looked at her askance, wondering what this woman was up to, "I'm not *lesbiana.*"

"Not even a little?" said Carmella.

"Well."

"You don't trust many people, do you?"

"I don't trust anybody. Isn't that sad?" said Lucha. "I don't trust my grandchild, I don't trust my neighbors, and I don't trust priests. I especially don't trust priests."

"Well, it's kind of normal not to trust priests, isn't it?" said Carmella.

Lucha allowed a faint smile, she almost liked this woman.

"What are you worried about? I can do a reading about you even if you aren't here. It's just better if you take part." said Carmella. "Come on, I'm just trying to be friendly."

"Alright." said Lucha reluctantly.

"Good."

Lucha watched closely as Carmella began to spread the cards out on the bench.

"I've never seen tarot cards like these."

"That's because I invented them."

"So, you've made your own tarot and I'm supposed to believe whatever you say it says?"

"Yeah, kind of crazy huh? You want me to stop?"

"No, keep going."

"Before we start, I want to come clean, It's best not to have secrets between us for the sake of the reading. I came over here because I see you here from time to time. You're not exactly friendly, but you're not horrible either."

"Well, thank you so much for pointing that out."

"But today you seem sadder than usual. I sense the power from you, but, even with such powers, you obviously despair like everyone else, maybe even more. I guess I'm just facinated to know why someone with your looks and power can't be happy, then it's senseless for the rest of us to even be concerned about it."

Carmella spread the deck of cards lengthwise on the bench, "First attract the card that shows the path you've been upon,... the past."

Using her hand as an instrument, Lucha held her outstretched hand over the cards with the intention of finding the past card.

"My compliments. This is a very powerful deck." said Lucha as she attracted the past card.

Carmella was encouraged that Lucha could sense the energy of the cards as she scanned the deck with her hand until one certain energy pattern stood out. With index finger extended, she lowered her hand, touched the card, pulled it from the pile and placed it face up.

Aztlánicon

"The *bruja*, thought so." said Carmella as she wrote down something on the small, vital notepad. She then returned the card to the pile and reshuffled it.

"Why do you do that? How do you build a spread if you return the card to the pile?"

"You just keep track on the notepad. This way the chaos can convey the same card more than once. All possibilities, at all times. Shall we keep going?" said Carmella.

"*Si.*"

"Next attract the card that shows where you are now, the present."

Lucha followed the same method to find the present card and placed it face up.

"The *Virgen*." said Carmella as she wrote it on the notepad.

"Let's keep going."

"Next attract the card that shows what approaches from the future."

Lucha pulled from the deck the future card and turned it over.

"A broken promise." said Carmella.

Lucha was startled by this and glared at the card. It was a blend of various odd shapes and colors, but it conveyed nothing in any language known to humans.

"How do you get a broken promise from.... that."

"It's the Card of Broken Promises."

"Says who?"

"Says me, it's my deck, I made it, it speaks to me." said Carmella. "Do you want to stop?"

"No, let's keep going."

"Alright, Where were we? A broken promise."

Carmella returned the future card to the deck and reshuffled. "Next attract the card that will show who has broken this promise."

Lucha closed her eyes, scanned the deck and pulled out the card of her intention.

"The Card of Present Company" said Carmella as she wrote it down. "Next attract the card that will show to who this promise was made."

Lucha already knew what that card would be. She scanned the deck anyway and pulled out,...

"The card of Ancestors" said Carmella."Now ask your questions. Say them out loud before you attract the card."

Lucha shifted her body and assumed a new focus. She considered what she might want to know.

"I attract the card that shows if the broken promise can be averted."

She scanned the deck and pulled out the card.

"The Way Out" said Carmella as she wrote it down.

Lucha was not sure if she wanted to know the way out? She couldn't imagine it would mean less responsibility than was already heaped upon her.

"To hell with it. I attract the card that shows the way out." said Lucha as she scanned the deck and pulled out the card.

"Birth." said Carmella.

Lucha was both intrigued and frightened. This card could govern what remains of her life.

"I attract the card that shows who gives this birth."

"The card of Present Company." said Carmella, she looked curiously at Lucha.

In an instant, Lucha knew why this woman was known to some as *Señora Iroñia*, with her probing personality and self-invented tarot deck that seemed infinitely changable, but, well suited to distilling meaning from chaos.

Lucha broke down and unleashed her troubles upon Carmella. She told her about the *linea divina*, the unjust murder of her Guadalupe Evangelina and the *pinche* priest that provoked their neighbors. About how Angélica refused initiation and her subsequent betrayal with the birth of *Jesus*, and the threat of Hector further weakening the bloodline of the Obregon women.

By the time Lucha came to a pause in her story, Carmella was dabbing away tears.

"No wonder you're so sad" said Carmella.

"Yes, I am. And aren't you glad that you know all about it now?"

"Yes, I am. I'm glad to know you Lucha Obregon." said Carmella, as she leaned over and hugged her.

"That's it, I'm ready to stop now." said Lucha wiping her eyes with both hands.

"Are you married?... or have a boyfriend?"

"No."

"Then, while we're here in contact with the realm, shouldn't you ask who the father should be?"

"It doesn't matter."

"Of course it matters. If it's the same father, she could have another boy, then what are you going to do?" said Carmella. "If you wait much longer, you may not be able to have another child."

"I'm not having another child, not at my age."

"You may not have a choice."

Lucha thought about it. She was right about asking the question. What could it hurt to see what the *energia* had to say?

"Alright. I attract the card that shows the father."

"The *Virgen*,... again." said Carmella.

"What does that mean?"

"I don't think it means that the *Virgen* will be the father."

"So, you're going to make jokes? This was your idea."

"Well, it could mean that you will meet the father here. Or perhaps, you will meet him on the *Dios de Guadalupe*."

"Or perhaps it means both. Perhaps it means neither."

"*Mujere*, you may not have enough time left. This initiation, as you called it. How old is that?"

"It depends,... maybe eight. Maybe older if she lacks capacity."

"Well, you'd better get on with it, *mujere*. Time is wasting. Instead of waiting at the mercy of your grand-daughter and her knuckle-dragger boyfriend, you should get your own child going. You'll double the odds of getting your *magica divina* child. Who knows, maybe you'll end up with two to carry on your lineage."

The Place of Miracles

They Possess Treasures Without Mercy

County Branciforte, California
December 12, 1995

"You can't kill a bishop." said Jimbo Arlington, as he drew his ancient persimmon driver back in the usual outside-in swing plane. He struck the ball sweetly and it sailed down the fairway. There was nothing like the sound of a well hit golfball, especially with real wood.

"Nice shot. You're finally starting to get a handle on that slice." said the Judge.

"Oh, thank you very much. I'm glad you approve. Let's see if you're so smug when I beat you today. You're going down. I feel a string of birdies coming on."

"I'm afraid it's 'bitter defeat' that you feel coming on." said the Judge as he sent the golfball down the middle of the fairway, until it faded around the sharp dogleg right.

"God damn you. Nice shot. That almost looked like you intended to do that."

"I did."

"Like hell."

Jimbo reached into his right pocket, pulled out a golfball and tossed it onto the tee box.

"A thousand dollars says you did not."

"What decides it?"

"It has to clear the bushes and not go into the creek." said Jimbo.

"Define 'clear the bushes'." said the Judge.

"The bushes must be between us and where the golfball ends up."

"So the bet is a thousand dollars that the bushes must be between us and where the golfball ends up.

"You're on." They shook hands.

The Judge teed up the golfball, then he stood quietly and took in the beautiful fairway. He gazed at the dog-leg and the area he wanted the ball to end up. He aligned his body and placed the club head slightly to the left of the target area. He drew the club away, coiled into position and then released his swing. The golfball sailed beautifully down the fairway, bounced in the intended area but continued on into the bordering creek.

"God damn. That's the first bet with you that's ever gone my way." said Jimbo.

"You didn't win the bet. I did."

"I said earlier that it had to stay out of the creek."

"Perhaps you did. But that's not what we shook hands on. We bet that the bushes would end up between us and the ball. The bushes are between us and the creek, correct? The ball is in the creek, correct?" said the merciless Judge as he held out his hand to be paid.

"Fuck. I'm stupid to bet against a lawyer."

"Always keep mindful of that, dear friend."

Jimbo pulled a money clip from his pocket and counted out ten one hundred dollar bills and handed them to the Judge.

"Hey, what's with the sweaty bills?"

"You deserve the sweaty bills."

"You carry a thousand dollars around with you?" said the Judge.

"We're playing golf aren't we?" said Jimbo as he walked back to the golf cart and got behind the wheel; the Judge placed his metal-driver into his golfbag and returned to the passenger seat and they drove away to the fifteen green that flirted with Painted Pony Lake.

As the golf cart approached the fifteenth green the air became filled with the pinched strumming of gut-string guitars and the rhythmic, insufficient thud of a *basso*. In the midst of it all floated the pitiful, unamplified voices shattered by blaring, storm-trooper horns.

"What's that racket?" said Jimbo.

"*Mariachis*. La Raza is celebrating *Dios de Guadalupe*."

"Celebrating? That noise would drive away normal people. And their blessed *Virgen*."

"Let them have their celebration while they can. It will all be gone soon enough." said the Judge. "So, back to the subject at hand. Technically, it's true that you can't kill a bishop. A bishop is what they refer to as a *corporation sole*, a corporation comprised of a single member. Since that single member is always a natural person, you can indeed kill the natural person. But, the tricky part is perpetual succession."

"You mean--- The King is dead, long live the King?" said Jimbo.

"Precisely. If we kill this one he will only be replaced by another."

"Yeah, but maybe the next one won't give a shit about any of this."

"That's a possibility. But with the Church suddenly threatening us with their patent rights on the Virgin Guadalupe, they could decide to escalate things and assert full property rights in the park. Then we'll have to fight them in court." said the Judge.

"That sounds expensive."

"Prohibitatively."

"But we could win."

"It'll take years. Cost millions."

"We're fucked."

"I suppose stalling is the only way out. And we do that by making the Bishop vanish"

"Are you sure?" said Jimbo.

"There'll be a period of confusion surrounding his disappearance, then they'll have to appoint a replacement. We'll wait until then to figure our next step." said the Judge.

"That patent bullshit steams my ass." said Jimbo. "Why didn't we think of that first?"

"I wish we had Jimbo." said the Judge. "I dearly wish we had."

"Yeah, we wouldn't be having the Bishop's death on our consciences."

They looked at each other and laughed.

Aztlánicon
CODEX I

∴ Ω ∴

Across the small lake, Lucha Obregon carefully held the hated *gringo* stroller so it didn't get away as she descended the slope to the 'place of miracles'. The smallish, natural amphitheater was clogged to capacity with *la gente*. The odd benches were filled to capacity. The fence protecting the *Virgen* had tranformed into a wall of flowers and pictures. In the middle of all of this, a line of pilgrims patiently waited to receive the priest's blessing.

Carmella Iroñia had suggested that this festival was the perfect opportunity to screen potential *bancos*. An attractive one, if possible. If the plan called for the exchange of bodily fluids, you may as well enjoy it as much as possible.

Lucha's belief system held that procreation was divinely intended to be enjoyable, enjoyable to an extreme. Otherwise, there never would have been enough takers willing to endure all of the trouble involved. A human species would never have evolved.

Lucha frantically pushed the stroller in search of sanctuary from the oncoming procession, which was put on every year by the diocese to flaunt their spiritual hegemony in the region. It took three full grown men to manage the painting of Virgin Guadalupe, she was a huge *gringo-ized* logo of colonized religion, considered a hostage by many in attendance.

There was nowhere to pull out, so Lucha continued precariously down the hill with the stroller containing *Jesus*. The procession had become long and narrow, due to the treacherous path that led down the hill. The concern on Lucha's face made it appear that she was being slowly chased by the captive Guadalupe logo.

Finally, Lucha reached the bottom of the path and pulled off to the side with *Jesus*. She dutifully made the sign of the cross as the Holy-Virgin logo passed by.

Eventually, six little girls passed by, each dressed like a little version of Frida Kahlo, ushered by three different mothers, all *mujeres* from the canning plant. With them was the proud Ernesto Saldano, night manager from the canning plant. Saldano was reputed to be an aging ladies man. Rumored to be involved with many women from the canning plant.

Lucha noticed that each of the girls took after her mother and they all seemed close in age, something that's entirely possible when you're not bogged down by the principle of monogamous mating. For Lucha, Ernesto seemed a perfect *banco*. He was of pleasant temperment, not bad to look at, but the most striking thing was that he had fathered all of these children and there was not a boy among them.

Once she settled upon Ernesto Saldano as the *banco*, Lucha wasted no time; she had no time to waste. In the late afternoon, when the sun was low in the west, after the three single-mothers had left with their little *Frida Kahlo* daughters, Lucha stalked Ernesto Saldano to make sure he didn't leave without her.

Ernesto happened upon a group of friends sitting around a tapped keg of *Cerveza Federales*. Lucha sat down and waited. *Cerveza Federales was* the favorite of no one. It was hauled out on certain holidays like *Dios de Guadalupe* and *cinco de mayo*. A reminder of the life left behind. After just a few cups, it was very easy to feel depressing shivers from their lives back in Mexico or Central America. The *aztlános* allowed themselves to get very drunk on *CF*.

Ernesto remained with the *borachos* until the sunlight had all but disappeared. Slowly he got up; said thank you and goodbye. As he made his way toward the parking lot, highly optimistic that he was competent to drive, Lucha decided it was time to make her move.

"Excuse me, *Señor* Saldano." said Lucha.

"Yes? Who's that?"

"Hi, It's me, Lucha Obregon from the canning plant."

It took him a moment to re-orient himself in the dim twilight, "Lucha. How are you? *Felice Dios de Guadalupe.*"

"Thank you. Could you help me? I'm sorry to ask, but, I left something back at the 'place of miracles' and I'm afraid to go back there alone. Could you go with me?"

"But it's getting dark."

"I have a flashlight."

Perhaps, if he hadn't drank several *ceverzas* accompanied by shots of *Respiro* tequila, it might not have made sense for Ernesto Saldano to go off in the dark with one of his employees, but, she apparently needed his help, and she was a good worker, and she was beautiful.

$$\therefore \Omega \therefore$$

Ernesto held the flashlight as Lucha pushed the *gringo* stroller in the lilting twilight, past the baseball diamond, past the empty soccer pitch and down the hill.

"Where are we going?" said Ernesto.

"We're almost there. Just another few minutes of your time, please."

"Are we going night fishing?"

When they got to the bottom of the hill, Lucha parked the stroller under the bilingual sign. Ernesto followed her with the beam of light as she walked to the base of the tree that bore the *milagro*. Lucha turned toward him and he looked at her with the flashlight. She reached down under her dress and pulled her panties down to her ankles. Ernesto's eyes widened, a sly grin came to his face.

"Turn out the light please." said Lucha as she leaned against the tree with her right hand and pulled the undergarment off the left leg, and then the right.

Ernesto turned off the flashlight and stepped toward her in the dimness, his hands reached out and found her clothed breasts. Lucha leaned back and kissed him tenderly.

"Would you please give me a girl?" she said.

"I'd sure like to try." said Ernesto.

Lucha reached down and withdrew his member, she fondled him to sufficiency. When the moment arrived, she placed both hands upon the bottom of the sacred *encina* tree. She drew the divine energy through her hands, through her arms, into her womb. As Ernesto drunkenly fumbled around his penetration, Lucha displayed to him an animal lust intended to encourage him and perhaps speed him along. Although he did not feel unpleasant inside of her, she was eager for him to inject her while she had the store of sacred *energia* within. Finally, Ernesto manifested the life-giving explosion and groaned loudly as he pumped his part of the bargain into her. Lucha leaned against the sacred tree, bent way over to encourage the sperm toward the womb. She mentally apprehended the *energia* coming from the *Virgen* and merged it with the energy going to her womb.

As Ernesto withdrew, he could tell that Lucha was occupied with concerns. He restored himself to a presentable state.

"Shall we get back up there?" he said.

"*Jesus* and I are going to sit here for a while with the *Virgen*." she said as she slowly straightened back up.

"I don't have a flashlight." said Ernesto.

"Take that one with you. I have another."

"Well, alright then. I guess I'll see you at work." he said.

"Yes, you will." she said as he turned to leave. "Ernesto, *gracias*."

"*De nada*, It was my pleasure dear lady. Any time I can be of service."

She watched the flashlight trail through the darkness as she moved to one of the benches, she laid down with her feet above her head, for the first time, the wild incline of the benches suddenly became both relevant and useful.

Aztlánicon
For Always A New Generation Cometh

∴ ⸙❧)Ω(☙⸙ ∴

For Always A New Generation Cometh
⸙⌒⌒⸙

1995
Waltonville, Aztlán

The mood was sullen among the tired and huddled working people in the southbound bus. They were being shuttled to the meager jobs that resulted from the first year of the *gringo's* NAFTA trade agreement. It took two buses to get from the aged tract houses of northside Waltonville across the river to the canning plant owned and operated by Quotidian Global. Many of those aboard had doubts that it was worth it to have left their families back home to tread water here in the promised land.

One of the dreary on the #75 was Angélica Obregon, who gently rocked *Jesus* in the *gringo* stroller in the aisle, which was against the rules. Lucha sat next to her on the bench seat, next to the window.

"I can't wait for him to outgrow that stroller." said Lucha.

"Nana, that will be soon enough. I can't wait for you to get off my back about this Obregon thing."

"Look, *m'jiha*, we both want this over with. Go and see him and tell him you want a girl. I told him about you. He'll do the rest. It will only take a few minutes."

"Oh, great. Only a few minutes. Don't build it up so much, Nana." said Angélica. "And what about Hector? What's he going to say about this?"

"Forget about that *Huévon.* By the time he gets out,

49

this will all be over."

"How old is this guy?"

"What difference does that make?"

"I don't want some old man crawling up inside of me."

"It can't be any worse than allowing that *babiche* Hector to fumble around in there."

Angélica let the comment pass. She'd grown used to Lucha's verbal barbs directed toward Hector. On the rare occasion that Hector was subtle enough to realize that he was being attacked, he was quite capable of speaking up on his own behalf. But, since he was away at one of the factory prisons, it didn't make any sense to get into it with her. Angélica returned to the subject at hand.

"He's old isn't he? How old?"

"It will just take a few minutes."

"He's old." said Angélica like a fact had just been established.

Poco despues, outside Ernesto Saldano's office, Lucha held the young child *Jesus* on her right hip as Angélica straightened herself up. She stopped when it occurred to her that she was preening herself for some old man. Angélica knocked on the door

"Yes?" said the voice from the other side.

Angélica opened the door and stepped inside.

Aztlánicon
For Always A New Generation Cometh

As Angélica closed the door she immediately locked it and turned around. She saw a middle-aged man with the thinest of black hair and a slight paunch in the belly. Angélica relaxed, it could be worse.

"Yes?" said Ernesto. "Can I help you?"

"I need a baby,... a girl baby." said Angélica.

Ernesto glared at her with no clue.

"She told me to tell you that I want a girl baby. That you would take it from there."

"Oh, you're Lucha's grand-daughter." said Ernesto. "She asked me something about the possibility of this, but I didn't think the crazy witch would actually do it."

"That's my Nana."

"Well, now is not a good time for this." said Ernesto.

"What's wrong with right now? It's only supposed to take a few minutes."

"Thank you. Thanks for the compliment."

Angélica moved some things on Ernesto's desk and then unbuttoned her pants. She smiled at Ernesto as she pulled them down to her knees and bent over the desktop and patiently presented herself to him. She closed her eyes and prayed that what she was about to do would be fruitful.

Seeing the beautiful young girl offered before him, a switch flicked in Ernesto and an immediate field of sex energy charged his aura and then dripped deliciously into his molecular body. He quietly stepped around behind her and caressed the small of her back, which turned into his finger lightly tracing the curves of her ample behind.

"You've got a wonderful ass, *querida*."

His hands slowly caressed her as though it was his privilege to sample a fine, rare wine.

"You've got wonderful hands." she said.

"If you don't mind, I'd like to take my time with you."

As his fingers gently focused on her sex, Angélica moaned, "Ahhh,... *manitas grata*. Take all the time you need."

Poco despues, Angélica emerged from Ernesto's office in a blissful haze, only to be jarred back to reality by the loud fussing of *Jesus*. Lucha could immediately sense that something had changed for Angélica, she had a gratified incandesence about her, an other-worldly quality in her eyes. Lucha and Angélica did not speak through the chilled drizzle, all the way back to the bus stop.

Seated next to her granddaughter on the crowded eastbound #75, Lucha spent the ride time back to the *barrio* mentally apprehending the fertile egg within Angélica's body. She visualized a divine girl child within the egg and imagined the symbols that would bringforth a mindstream therein. Lucha radiated a beam of intention, pulling the viscious spermatazoa toward the egg of the chosen one. Once she sensed the presence of the sperm at the egg wall, Lucha released her grasp. She had no desire to experience the raw violence that is so innocently known as fertilization. As Lucha returned to the waking state, she slowly opened her eyes and remembered that her molecular body was on the bus.

"Where were you just now?" said Angélica.

"I was helping along the *concepcion* of your daughter."

"Stay out of my body, Nana."

Many heads turned their way.

"*Quietate, m'hija*"

The two of them remained silent for a few moments, until the weirdness passed, Lucha decided to change the subject.

"So it wasn't so bad?" said Lucha.

"It wasn't bad at all."

"Good. Hopefully a ripe baby girl will result from this."

"Hopefully, it won't. "

"Why do you say that?"

"I don't want to get pregnant right away. It would be best if it took several attempts." said Angélica.

"*M'hija*, it's best if we get on with this."

"For God's sake, Nana. Since I'm doing what you want, is it so bad that I might enjoy a little bit of it?"

Lucha knew that her granddaughter was right.

"Alright, *m'hija*. But, you'll keep trying until you get pregnant?"

"Every chance I get, Nana. Every chance I get."

Aztlánicon
For Their Sakes Came The Flood

For Their Sakes Came The Flood

1978
Ciudad Obregon, Sonora, Mexico

Eight years into the secret *ocupacion de Aztlán*, the people of the states of Sonora and Chihuahua braced for another reign of terror upon their *magica divina*. It was a dark and tumultuous time, like it always was whenever there was a shift in the hierarchy of the church.

Upon the death of the beloved Cardinal Madrigal, an irksome vacancy had arisen within the pontifical senate. The vacancy was irksome because whoever was chosen to wear the scarlet birretta would surely be eager to leave his mark upon his jurisdiction. After all, it would be foolish to squander the brief window of fame a new Cardinal would attract, especially now that the current Bishop of Rome was very old and in the midst of failing health. The new Cardinal would not only have a *vocé en conclave*, but would also be in the field of candidates from which the new Pontiff would be elected.

Cortéz the suffragan languished in the thick, sweltering heat that smothered the cathedral courtyard that August. He was there by subpoena of his archbishop, on matters not his privilege to know. He sat and thumbed his rosary and recounted shallow prayers until the nonlocality of the moment collapsed as the attendent swung open the door.

"His Grace will see you now."

Cortéz the suffragan followed the attendent under a trellis threaded with long slender succulents and numerous prickly flowers that provided nothing in the way of shade. The two celebates walked in silence around the cathedral until they came to the threshold of the axial chapel.

"Go right in."

Cortéz was staggered as he stepped into the chapel. He had never seen anything it's equal. It was lavish with European paintings and sculptures of a glorious, religious nature. Even the collection of meso-american artifacts would humble the national museums of Mexico City. At the heart of the chapel was the tabernacle, the glorious container the Catholics reserved for the presence of God. Gently leaning on the tabernacle was the infamous Archbishop Carlotta, in mystical communion with the portion of God inside.

Mindful that a humble young priest waits to be invited to sit in the presence of an archbishop, Cortéz endured the string of awkward moments until the mind of the grand man returned to the realm of mere mortals. The Archbishop was momentarily incapacitated in the shift back to particle consciousness. Permission to sit was gestured. Cortéz walked across the room, took a seat and watched the archbishop commune with his *confidente* God, all stooped over, he whispered to it like there was some faery being kept inside. Cortéz felt like applauding to keep the feary alive, but he thought better of it and kept that to himself.

Again, the Archbishop re-emerged within the human dimension and slowly turned his attention to Cortéz.

"My son, as you probably know, we have a new Cardinal."

"Yes, your Excellency. I've heard that."

"What you may not have heard is that the new Cardinal is wasting no time in campaigning for Pontiff."

"I haven't heard that, Your Grace."

Aztlánicon
For Their Sakes Came The Flood

"Of course you haven't. You're only a priest."

Cortez was surprised that the Archbishop would be so illustrative of their class differential. Something you'd expect from a lesser person, not someone of a *sangre azul* lineage. Perhaps the Archbishop was just sensitive from being passed over for Cardinal, yet again. Carlotta was bitter to be stalled in middle management; his bloodline deserved better, far better.

"As with all who have an eye toward becoming Pontiff," said the archbishop, "The new Cardinal feels that things need to be stirred up."

"Stirred up, Your Grace?"

"He feels the authority of the Church is weakened by the presence of witches and practicioners of these damned indigenous religions."

Cortéz let the silence sit there, contributing nothing, until he finally said, "I'm not sure what you're asking of me, Your Excellency."

"Do you realize what these indigenous religions mean to the Holy Church?"

"No sir."

"Lost market share. That's what."

"That's most regrettable, Your Excellency."

"Not as regrettable as having His Eminence point out that right under my nose there are villages in Sonora where witchcraft is practiced openly."

"Openly?"

"Yes, openly. With no fear of reprisal."

"Are you asking me to put the fear of reprisal in the people, Your Excellency?"

"Not the fear of reprisal,... reprisal itself."

For several months, Cortéz the suffragan wandered the state of Sonora, searching for witchcraft being practiced openly. Eventually word came that he'd been summoned back to Ciudad Obregon to report to the Archbishop.

"Your Excellency, I'm happy to report to you that church attendance has picked up and that I have scoured the countryside and the practice of witchcraft and native religions seems to have ceased completely."

"Bumpkin. How do I prove that to His Eminence?"

"How can we prove something doesn't exist, your Excellency?"

"The Cardinal will say people are pretending until you go away. I need proof for him that will overcome all doubt."

"I'm afraid I'm not subtle enough to know what that would be, your Excellency."

"How many *brujas* have been turned in?"

"Not one, your Excellency. But I took that to mean that we were successful in quashing the practice."

"It doesn't matter what you took it to mean. It all depends upon how it looks to His Eminence. What you've done so far only proves that you've accomplished nothing or worse."

"Worse, your Excellency?"

"Far worse. It might prove that there wasn't even a problem to begin with."

Aztlánicon
For Their Sakes Came The Flood

"How is that worse, your Excellency? Isn't it good if we don't have the problem?"

"This mission was given by the Cardinal. This was all his idea. Do you want to spend your time and energy proving that the new Cardinal had a stupid idea? "

"I see your point."

"This calls for extraordinary measures."

"Your Excellency, I am here to accomplish any task in order to serve God." said Cortéz.

"You're not here to serve God. You're here to serve me."

Cortez was stunned by that bit of information and as bitter as it was, he swallowed it.

"Yes, Your Excellency."

The Archbishop indicated a Bible on a stand next to the suffragan. "A wonderous tool, the Bible. Justification for almost anything can be found between it's covers. Open it to the Book of Exodus,.... chapter twenty-two."

The priest did as instructed.

"Now, read verse seventeen."

The priest traced his finger down the page.

"Thou shall not let a sorceress live." Cortez took a moment to reflect. "I'm not clear about what you're asking of me, sir. Do you want me to go out and kill witches?"

"I'm a archbishop of the Holy Church, for Christ's sake. I can't give you any such an order."

Cortéz wasn't sure where this was going, he decided

to wait for the Archbishop to clarify.

"Besides you needn't kill anyone directly. You merely facilitate bringing it about. We need something tangible to show His Eminence that his mission has been accomplished."

"You mean that it will only look accomplished if someone is executed?"

"What's more tangible than a dead body?"

"Couldn't it look like we simply selected someone as a scapegoat?"

"That's why the people of Sonora have to turn over one of their own. It's the only thing that will show a healthy fear has taken root. Then I'll have something to take to His Eminence."

"But, your Grace, I've been at this for months and no one has been turned in. How can I go to make this happen?" said the priest.

"Go in disguise to a place where you haven't exposed yourself. Find someone vulnerable. Just pick someone. And then apply the pressure. Keep applying it until they give someone up. If they fail to accuse anyone,... then they're obviously hiding someone. They've condemned themselves. But, let me be very clear. Pick someone and carry out Exodus 22:17."

The priest suddenly felt awkward, this wasn't why he became a priest. He didn't know what to say, so he said nothing.

"Don't worry, my son. Have faith." said the grand man. "We must be tireless in our efforts to maintain the one True Faith."

Aztlánicon
For Their Sakes Came The Flood

Aldea Católica, Sonora
December, 1978

Josefina Amarrete was deeply concerned when the stranger appeared at her door. She foolishly allowed him in. Only the day before the small cup imbued with the spirit of the *orisha* had fallen from the tiny shelf where it had been placed by the village *babalawo*. Josefina failed to understand that the cup's plummet was Osun's warning of impending danger.

She poured the tea blended from local chaparral and watched the stranger try not to look uneasy. He slowly hoisted the cup to his lips and sniffed. He glanced at her to see if she was watching and he pretended to taste it.

"Very good, but too hot." he said as he set down the cup.

She looked at him askance and pointed to a large glass urn on the rustic table.

"It's December. It's sun tea."

"Is it medicinal?" he said, trying to change the subject.

She reasoned that he probably thought he was being poisoned. He was obviously deceitful and seemed to have reason to anticipate the worst. His reason for being here must surely be a lie.

"I don't really know of such things." she said.

Josefina was overcome with the urge to flee. There had been murmurs of a priest who appeared from nowhere, asking nosy questions about local *hecherias* and people that practice *magica divina*. Josefina wasn't sure if this stranger was this priest, but he sure wasn't the writer from Mexico City he pretended to be.

"Do people go to *hecherias* because they fear reprisals if they don't?" said the stranger.

"Do you mean, do people feel forced to go to *hecherias* like they feel forced to go to the Church?"

The stranger fought to maintain the persona.

"Yes, do they feel forced?"

"Hardly. People go to them for many things. Healings, droughts, protective spells, things like that." she said.

"Do you go to *hecherias*?" said the stranger.

"No. I have no need." she said.

"Why is that? Do you practice the *magica divina* yourself?"

Josefina indicated an altar in the corner of the room, upon it a primitive carving of the *Virgen de Guadalupe*.

"Of course not. I have the *Virgen* watching over me." she said.

"Of course, the *Virgen de Guadalupe*. So then, the *Virgen* helps you with healings, droughts, things like that?"

Josefina feared where this was going. She realized that she must derail this conversation, or, at least, switch tracks.

"You know, I could tell you what you want to know about those who practice the *magica divina*. Of course, it would be at great personal risk. Then you would go back to Mexico City and write your book, and where would I be then?"

"So, it's money that you want?" said the stranger.

Aztlánicon
For Their Sakes Came The Flood

"Money would be nice, but there is something else."

"And what would that be?"

Josefina moved closer with a playful expectancy in her air.

"I'm a woman, living alone. I occasionally have needs." she said as she reached out and fluently traced his inner thigh all the way up.

The stranger twitched slightly and began to swell under her gentle touch. He lingered in her pleasurable offering until he recognized a shift in the balance of power. He abruptly backed away.

"How did you know?"

"I wasn't sure. I just knew you weren't who you said you were. So, should I call you Father?"

"That's the tradition." said the priest. "So will you help me?"

Josefina again reached out and lightly played with his swollen-ness. "You know the offer still stands, even if you are a priest."

The priest reached down and seized her by the wrist, he held it aloft in a most threatening manner.

"It may appear to you that you have me at a disadvantage, but, let me assure you, it only appears that way. Will you help me?"

"Perhaps." said Josefina.

"Perhaps?" said the priest, visably angry. "Well, then, will you help yourself?"

Josefina's demeanor changed instantly, there was no trace of playfulness, the sexual tension had evaporated.

"Now that you've found me out, I may as well settle for you." said the priest.

"Not me. You don't want me."

"Then who do I want? Give me a name."

Josefina desperately considered who she could give up.

"Come now, there must be someone you can think of."

"Guadalupe."

"That's not good enough. There must be a thousand Guadalupes around here."

"Guadalupe Evangelina Obregon, she's the one you want." said Josefina. "Everyone knows she practices *magica divina.*"

✝

Aldea Católica, Sonora
December, 1978

On the morning of the appointed day, the crowd assembled at the holocaust site on the outskirts of the small, noble village. There was growing disappointment for those that brought big rocks, there were too many people to get close enough to hit the beautiful witch while she was still alive. They managed their disappointment in the knowledge that they had come all this way only to participate symbolically. Some of those gathered were neighbors of the condemned witch, local villagers who had no quarrel with the *bruja*, but, if the priest said her execution will cleanse the darkness that had overshadowed their village and end the drought, then so be it. Some in the mob were there because they feared witches. Some because they were witches and didn't want to be found out. Some because human sacrifice had echoed through the region for ages and they would never

Aztlánicon
For Their Sakes Came The Flood

pass up an opportunity to be a party to one.

The priest nervously hovered around the young woman, keeping the mob at bay. It was obvious that, even though this was all his doing, he was ill at ease with what was about to take place.

Guadalupe Evangelina Obregon was lashed to a *ceiba* tree with a coarse rope that dug into her wrists. She didn't dwell upon the pain, nor did she imagine the unimaginable pain in store for her, that would manifest soon enough. Nor did she dwell upon the terrible question of what would become of her infant child. Nothing could be done about that now. Instead, she spent those final moments with the aromas of the sage and mesquite, and the exotic buzzing of the locusts in the thick air. She allowed her universe to be consumed in the magical context of the moment. The priest stepped forward, the crowd stirred.

"God said unto Moses, You shall not let a sorceress live." said the priest. "Guadalupe Obregon, you have turned your back on the edicts of God and his Holy Church and you have chosen to live as a sorceress."

"I live exactly as God made me." said the raven-haired beauty.

"Do not blaspheme further, child, spare yourself further pain. God did not make you like this."

"God has made everything exactly as it is, priest, exactly as it is." said Guadalupe.

"Even now, you blaspheme against the teachings of the Holy Church, the one true faith."

"My faith is in God, not in the Church." she said so that all could hear.

There were scattered gasps throughout the crowd, shock that she would say something like that in public. The priest turned to the assembled.

"You see? She openly blasphemes against the Church."

"Why do you try and stand between me and my God, priest?" she said.

"You cannot know God, except through the grace of the Holy Church" said the priest. "But instead, you dwell outside her loving refuge and practice the evil craft."

"Many here practice the *magica divina*." said Guadalupe.

Several in the crowd gasped. The priest bristled at the new opportunity that had arisen. He slowly turned and faced the crowd.

"Point them out, so that we may know who they are."

Guadalupe could feel the fear that swept through the crowd, it was palpable, it was manifest. She scanned the gathering of enemies and neighbors as though she was going to give someone up to the priest at any moment. Many of the assembled foolishly averted their faces, which only served to point themselves out.

Arturo Valenzuela, the village *santero* stepped to the fore. Now that he'd made himself known, it was unlikely that anyone would dare to do anything. The *babalawo* slowly strolled around the condemned as he appeared to search for a good place to aim. He halted directly in front of the *bruja*, with the priest behind her.

"Yes, *bruja*. Point them out to us." said the *santero*.

At that moment a rock came flying in and struck Guadalupe's left collar bone. She doubled over, held up only by the tether, her wind knocked out.

Arturo jumped in front of her, "Who did that?"

Aztlánicon
For Their Sakes Came The Flood

The crowd was silent, except for a lone voice, "Careful Arturo, we could hit you and the priest if you don't get out of the way."

The energy of bloodlust swirled through the crowd. Cortez recognized that it had gone too far to control. He began to back away.

As Guadalupe Evangelina hung from the tree, she knew the door to this life was closing for her if she didn't do something right now. She swung her legs under her and tried to get up. As she slowly stood in her extreme pain, she aligned her being with the names of God.

"*Ai,... Jah,.... Vau.*"

She opened herself to the indwelling God.

"*Ai,.... Jah,.... Vau.*"

A mist of the conscious ether slowly began to envelop the assembled as Guadalupe Evangelina aligned herself further. Cortéz was caught unawares.

"*Ai,.... Jah,.... Vau.*" said Guadalupe, as she gave way fully to the indwelling God. She intoned, "Save me, O God, by thy name, and judge me by thy strength. Hear my prayer, O God; give ear to the words of my mouth."

"What the hell is this?" said Cortéz.

"For strangers are risen up against me, and oppressors seek after my soul: they have not set God before them. *Se-lah.*"

Cortéz recognized a Psalm when he heard one. He realized what she was doing. It must stop at any cost.

"Kill her. What are you waiting for?" said Cortéz to the *babalawo.*

Guadalupe Evangelina continued, "Merciful *Obatalá,* please keep your promise to me. *Omo-Obatalá, Omo-*

Obatalá"

"Kill her, now! Be done with it." yelled Cortéz.

"Mine eye hath seen his desire upon mine enemies." said Guadalupe, as the crowd began to speak the words *Omo-Changó, Omo-Changó.*

Amid the growing chant, the *babalawo* stiffened abruptly under the shadow of the indwelling God, *Changó.*

Cortéz realized that all was lost if the witch didn't die this minute. He turned to the crowd.

"I order you in the name of the Church. Stone her. Do it now!"

The *babalawo* reached back and hurled the jagged rock over the witch and hit Cortez on the right temple with a sickening thud. His skull snapped back with horrific force and his body collapsed to the ground. A deluge of jagged, painful rocks rained down on Cortéz. As the crowd slowly filed by, more and more rocks fell on the pile until the body could no longer be seen.

In the aftermath, Arturo felt light-headed and thirsty, but, he managed his way over to the beautiful, injured witch and cut her loose. She collapsed into his arms with a mortal groan. The *babalawo* then turned to the crowd.

"Whoever you are. I've got the rock you threw. If you don't make yourself known. I will find you in the ether this very night. You will not live to see another sun."

From the crowd rushed a snivelling little man who had much to protect. "Please I'm sorry. I'm very sorry. I was afraid she was going to reveal me."

"What is there about you that is worth revealing. You carry her back to the village."

Aztlánicon
For Their Sakes Came The Flood

As the crowd traipsed behind, uncertain as to what came over them, they were thankful that a serious threat to their *magica divina* was now just a pile of jagged rocks.

uncertain as to what came over them,...

Aztlánicon
CODEX II

⠂⠄⠆⠈ ꞊ꞏꞍ) Ω (꞊ꞏꞍ ⠈⠆⠄⠂

In Malediction Shall Be Thy Portion

Sonora, Estados Unitos de Mexico

1978

The juicy energy of human sacrifice hung in the air of MesoAmerica for millenia, the gods willed it, the gods that were concocted so that the creatures might have a *creator*. It was that way before the *aztecas*, before the *toltecas*. And then the Europeans came and sprayed the land with *español* and unleashed a voracious church upon the poor inhabitants and their *magica divina*.

It should have been obvious to Lucha Obregon that a woman from her matrilineage would be blamed for the long drought. Especially since there were rumors of a priest lurking in the background, canvassing for scapegoats, pressing the people until someone would finally be given up. How could Lucha not recognize that conditions had deteriorated to that point? The general custom demanded that something be put to death. The local custom was that it be an Obregon woman.

While the engine idled, an old Ford pickup sat on a small hill that overlooked the holocaust site. Lucha Obregon fought the unbearable urge to watch the execution of her daughter. Who could bear such memories going through their mind for the rest of their life?

Lucha 's fingers lightly grazed the *sceptre* that leaned against the dashboard, the *sceptre* that embodied the matrilineage of Obregon women. The *scepter* that she always thought she'd pass on to her daughter. She looked down at the infant she held in her arm and already regretted the immense burden now placed upon such a small child, the final hope of the matrilineage.

It was a mystical capacity that passed from mother to daughter, secreted in the blood of Obregon women. The *scepter* signified the burden to preserve the matrilineage. It passed to Lucha upon her mother's death. Although the practice of *magica divina* had been cultivated in her daughter, Lucha could not pass her the *scepter* because she never conveyed the necessary gnosis empowerments. It now seemed the time for that had passed.

Lucha envisioned Guadalupe Evangelina within an orb of golden radiance, the radiance of the *Virgen*. A shaft of diamond light extended from below her, through the length of her and above her, from earth-star to soul-star and all of the vortexes in between. Lucha abided with this vision.

"*No jodas! Mira aqui!*" said Ramon Sanchez, from behind the steering wheel, "*Putamadre*, they stoned the priest!"

Lucha kept her attention focused on the vision of Guadalupe Evangelina being protected by the *Virgen*.

"How is Guadalupe?"

"She looks hurt, but still alive."

Lucha turned to look as the crowd below dispersed. She saw her injured Guadalupe Evangelina being carried, the villagers plodding behind. Lucha gave thanks for the *Virgen's* intervention. It must have saved her daughter. She looked at the pile of jagged rocks that now rested upon the corpse. The priest would receive no funeral, not even a burial. The body would be dragged into the hills and left to the animals. At least some good would come from the Exodus Agenda.

"She's still alive." said Ramon. "This complicates

things."

"Let's go get her."

"I'm supposed to get you and the child all the way up to *Magdelena*."

"The child? Don't you mean your daughter?" said Lucha.

"We don't know that that's my child."

"So like most men, your responsibility ends when you zip up your pants?"

"I like that. I'm going to use it." said Ramon.

As the old Ford pickup weaved along the federal highway, north of Guaymas, it was all Ramon Sanchez could do to keep the worn out old truck on the roadway. The bench seat was crowded by the gravely injured Guadalupe, sprawled over the middle, lying mercifully unconscious. Lucha was pressed against the door with the infant child fidgiting in her arms.

"The deal was to deliver you and the child to the *coyotes*. Not her. She's already spoken for." said Ramon.

Lucha wished she had something heavy to crush his skull, but it was convenient to let him drive them, she needed to meet up with the *coyotes* and hopefully the three of them could disappear into the promised land of Aztlán.

"You greedy pig. Just get us to *Magdelena*. I'll get you more money later." she said.

"Guadalupe stays here with me. That was the deal with the priest."

"The priest is dead. The deal is off."

"The deal is not off. They will send other priests."

"How can you do this? She's the mother of your child."

"How many times do I have to tell you?"

"Guadalupe is coming north with me. And that's final." said Lucha.

The pickup stopped in the middle of the deserted highway. Ramon flung open the door and jumped out into the glorious Sonoran sunrise. He leaned in, grabbed Guadalupe and jerked her out, over his shoulder. She screamed in horrible pain. As Lucha instinctively reached out for her daughter, the infant began to cry. Lucha placed her on the bench seat and slid behind the steering wheel.

Outside, Ramon hurled Guadalupe into the truck bed like a bag of cement. Again, she screamed in pain. With strictly business detachment, Ramon pulled a revolver from the small of his back and shot Guadalupe in the face, twice.

"There. End of discussion." he said.

Lucha gasped as she realized what had just happened. She watched as Ramon returned the revolver to the small of his back and climbed into the truck bed to rearrange some things to conceal the body. Lucha quietly pressed down on the clutch pedal, as she looked over at the screaming child, she gently pulled the column shift toward her and down. She wiped her eyes while she watched Ramon in the rearview mirror.

"Shut that fucking brat up." he said as he stood up, facing forward.

Lucha released the clutch, jammed on the gas pedal and the truck lunged forward. Ramon fell backward and landed on the roadway. As the truck sped off, Ramon slowly staggered to his feet and pulled out the revolver and fired twice.

Lucha heard the first shot, it must have missed the truck entirely. The second shot pierced the rear and passenger windows, Lucha looked over and saw the child covered with glass, glass was everywhere. Lucha wiped the tears from her swollen eyes as she drove what was left of the Obregon matrilineage toward the promised land. She knew that she could keep herself composed at least until *Magdelena* to meet the *coyotes*. Perhaps then there would be enough time for her to fall apart.

74

Adrift In Thy Promised Land

1994
County Branciforte, Aztlán

Lucha Obregon remained vigilant for the signs that were never to come. Her plans for passing down the *magica divina* to the next generation were butchered by living among the *gringos*. Angélica had grown into a beautiful young *pocha* and showed no inclination toward the ancient pathway that abided in her blood.

Despite Angélica's bitter indifference, Lucha stubbornly continued to perform the initiation rituals in the desperate hope of arousing the *serpent energy* enbedded within the would-be initiate.

"I can only get you so far, *m'hija*, you've got to help out, you have to at least try." said Lucha.

"Nana, Why are you bothering with this? I'm not like you, I'm not a *bruja*." said Angélica.

"Captive bird, belief is thy cage." said Lucha.

"Nana, you want me to believe in something I just don't believe in. Magic isn't real. These are modern times."

"Magick isn't real?" said Lucha "Then why did the priest seek the death of your poor mother? And why did I have to run away with you and come up here to live among the *gringos*?"

"Well, excuse me for not being in a hurry to get

stoned to death. And living among the *gringos* hasn't been so bad, has it?

"Just look at you *m'jiha*." said Lucha. "You've become a *pocha*. You've given up on our ways."

"I just want to live like a normal person. What is wrong with that?"

"You're not a normal person, *m'jiha*. If your poor mother could see you like this."

"If my mother could see me like this? She'd be happy for me to be exactly as I am." said Angélica.

Lucha hated it when her granddaughter aired such disrespect, but, she knew of no good remedy for the attitude, especially from someone with such a strong will. If Angélica was cold toward the *magica divina*, forcing her involvement would only fetch *caotica*, and hasten the extinction of the matrilineage.

"Alright, *m'jiha*, you win. I'm not going to waste anymore time with you."

"Oh, thank you Nana, *graçious*." said Angélica as she reached out and hugged Lucha.

Lucha graciously welcomed the hug from her grand-daughter, but, business remained undone. Lucha lovingly pulled away and took the girl by the shoulders and looked straight into her eyes.

"You're not off the hook, not even close. You now owe the matrilineage a girl, an Obregon girl to take your place." said Lucha.

"I owe the lineage a girl? What am I, a baby factory?" said Angélica.

"You are now. Don't be frightened *m'jiha*, It's only a baby girl or two." said Lucha.

"Why two?" said Angélica.

"If the first doesn't take to the Obregon magick, like you didn't. It's not unthinkable that your daughter might take after you."

"That could take years."

"This is true, that's why we must get started right away. On your knees." said Lucha.

Angélica stood in disbelief for a moment, until she realized that her grandmother was serious.

"Nana, this is what I mean. On your knees? This isn't normal."

Lucha closed her eyes and took several slow, deep breaths. With each exhalation she merged her being with the *serpent energy*. She slowly opened her eyes and looked gently upon her grandchild. Angélica hated it when Nana got like this. These were the times when magick was the most convincing, when Nana stood there absorbed in the energy of generations of *brujas*. You could feel it from her eyes. It filled the room.

"Fuck it." said Angélica as she lowered to her knees.

"The blood that flows though you binds you to produce an heiress to our matrilineage. Do you accept this pledge to produce an heiress?"

"I do."

"So be it."

Angélica Obregon took seriously her promise to her grandmother and the matrilineage. In the following months she presented herself to several *bancos* until one of the seeds took root within her. At the ripe age of fourteen, Angélica fell with child, possibly the last hope of the Obregon matrilineage. Lucha Obregon, now forty-five, anxiously awaited the coming of her great-grand-daughter. Being well versed in indigeneous midwifery, Lucha was to perform the delivery when the joyous time arrived.

"There's the crown, *m'jiha*, ... we're almost there. Now, deep breath, now, pushshshsh." said Lucha.

Lucha had to turn the baby's head gently to allow one shoulder to clear. Lucha struggled to keep her balance as she slid in with both hands to catch the baby.

"Good job, *m'jiha*." said Lucha as she stood up with the newborn. Then she saw the penis. "A boy! *Putamadre*. What the hell am I going to do with a boy?"

This was the bitterest of moments for Lucha, she looked at the beautiful, useless male child. She glared at the exhausted Angélica.

"If we were back home, we would leave him outdoors overnight and if he was still there in the morning, then we'd bother to raise him."

Lucha saw that he was helpless and tried not to love him. She placed the whimpering infant onto the chest of his exhausted mother and managed her disappointment enough to tend to the delivery of the placenta and cleaning up of the mess.

"You rest now, *m'jiha*, You'll recover, and we'll get you ready for the next one." said Lucha.

"The next one?" said Angélica, breathless.

"Yes, *m'jiha*, You still owe us a girl."

"It would have been easier to just learn the damned magick." said the exhausted Angélica.

"Probably, *m'jiha*, but, we'll never know. Now that

you've renounced *magica divina*, I couldn't teach you if I wanted to." said Lucha. "I swore to our matrilineage that I would never pass the *linea* to someone unworthy."

"Now I'm going to be a mother of two before I'm old enough to drive."

"As if you could ever afford to drive." said Lucha.

"It would have been easier to just learn the damned magick."

Aztlanicon

Amidst The Offspring Of The Ungodly

1994
Waltonville, Aztlán

7 WHEN A MAN SELLS HIS DAUGHTER AS A SLAVE,
SHE SHALL NOT GO FREE AS MALE SLAVES DO.
--- EXODUS 21 :

In the aftermath of the disasterous birth of *Jesus,*
Lucha Obregon's family languished in an old housing
tract on the outskirts of the small rural town. During
those bitter months that followed Angélica's betrayal,
Lucha could only stand by and watch as the heiress to the
matrilineage fell in with a very rough crowd. Lucha kept
her eye on one *macho hombre* in particular, Hector
Huevón, a worthless male if there ever was one.

Lucha was certain that Huevón fathered *Jesus*, but he
would never admit to it. It was rumored that he'd sired
many children in the region and provided support for
none of them. No one would dare report Hector as a
deadbeat-dad, if they did they would disappear. It would
be said that they probably had gone back to Mexico.
Who would there be to dispute it?

"*M'jiha*, don't cover your face with all of that make-
up." said Lucha, bitter that Angélica had turned her back
on the *magica divina* and become lost to the ways of the
pochos.

"Nana! You're driving me crazy!" said Angélica.

"Don't yell at me *m'jiha*. I don't respond well to
being yelled at."

Angélica was well aware of everything that was implied in her grandmother's statement. It was never good to confront her directly, her will usually prevailed.

"Sorry." she said with obvious contrition. "Nana please. Hector likes me like this. And if he likes it, that's the way it's going to be."

$$\therefore \Omega \therefore$$

Lucha watched as Angélica sat in a corner of the room, with her back to everyone. Around her left arm was a belt pulled tight with her teeth. Lucha turned away, she couldn't watch as Angélica seemed overcome by *heroina,* her head tilted back as she slowly collapsed into the chair.

Lucha picked up the baby *Jesus* and put him into the *gringo* stroller. Lucha hated that stroller, but she still used it for the long walk to the place of miracles.

"*Jesus* and I are going to the lake." said Lucha. "I don't want him to see you like this, *m'hija.*"

Angélica barely stirred, her eyes half open and unfocused.

"Nana, please call him *Chuy.* I'm trying to get him used to it."

"Why name him *Jesus* if you're going to call him Chuy?"

"Because that's just what people do, Nana. Look, I don't want to talk about this now." said Angélica barely able to keep her eyes open.

"Yeah grandma," said Hector, who was sprawled over the couch in his warm-ups and wife-beater. "Come on, they even do that in Mexico."

"Mark my words, *m'jiha,* these new *pocho* ways aren't going to serve you well." said Lucha.

"Mark my words" mocked Hector. "You're always trying to come off like Yoda or some shit. Why don't you cut out the *magica divina* bullshit and let my woman be who she wants to be?"

Lucha turned toward him. "Your woman? So, you're admitting that *Jesus* is your son?"

"I didn't say that."

"If you are not the child's father,... then how is the child's mother your woman?" said Lucha. "And, if you are not the child's father, then what business is it of yours what we call him?"

Hector backed off. This *mujere* made her displeasure known in ways that just weren't normal. That didn't mean he'd ever admit to being afraid of her. She was only a woman, after all.

"Fuck all of this *magica* bullshit." Hector said.

"You should not talk about the *magica divina* in that manner." said Lucha. "The *energia* elevates the lowly, but, brings down the elevated."

"What the fuck is that supposed to mean, Yoda? Are you saying that I'm not elevated? I'm higher than a *putamadre*."

Angélica couldn't help but chuckle.

Lucha just smiled as though there was nothing to say. The intended insult did not go over Hector's head.

"Hey, fuck you if you can't take a joke, *mujere*."

Angélica turned and slaped Hector hard across the face.

"Don't you dare disrespect my Nana."

Aztlanicon
Amidst The Offspring Of The Ungodly

Hector was stunned that the young girl would do that. His reaction was to backhand her, hard; but he'd been through the legal system before for doing precisely that.

"Yeah, why don't you take Chuy to the lake, grandma." he said and then turned and sprawled out on the sofa once more.

Lucha knew there was not much sense in talking with Angélica while she was on the *heroina*.

"We'll see you later."Lucha stopped and turned to Angélica."*M'jiha*, come outside a second."

As Lucha pushed the stroller through the door, Hector couldn't leave well enough alone and called out, "Maybe you'll see a *milagro* or some shit, grandma."

Angélica glared at Hector, telling him to shut up with her half open eyes. She slowly got up and followed her grandmother outside.

"If you are going to lie down with that *pendejo*,... you use a *condón*." said Lucha.

"I thought you wanted me to get pregnant?"

"Not with that *cretino*. Not while you're a *yonqui*."

"Alright." said Angélica.

"Do you promise me, *m'jiha*? This is *muy importante*."

Angélica nodded with indistinct, half-opened eyes. Lucha grabbed her by the sholders to get her attention.

"Let me hear you say it." said Lucha.

"I promise."

"You promise what?"

"I promise that we'll use a *condón*, Nana."

"I'm going to the *Virgen* to seek guidance about a suitable *banco*." said Lucha as she turned with the *gringo* stroller. "Go and lay down before you fall down."

"Yes, Nana." said Angélica, gently swaying.

Hector emerged from hiding in the hallway.

"Bye grandma. Say hello to the *Virgen* for me." he said

Hector's arm was around Angélica as they stood watching Lucha push the stroller down the street. Angélica's eyes were no longer half-closed.

"Do you think it worked?" said Angélica.

"Don't know yet."

"Stop mocking her."

"I'm just playing with her while she's up on her high horse."

"You should be careful. She can play with you right back. Worse if you push her."

Hector lightly smacked Angélica on the back of the head, just enough to get her attention.

"You better not slap me like that when we're alone." he said. "That shit was viscious."

Angélica leaned over and kissed him, "I'm sorry baby. You were dissing her right in front of me. If I didn't do something, she would think that I've turned against her."

"What do we care if she thinks we're against her?

"I'm just trying to get out of having another baby. I don't need to turn my grandmother into an enemy."

"What enemy? She's a woman."

"If you cross her and make her your enemy, she will take your life force away. Not that you're doing much with it."

"She can do that?"

"In her spare time. While watching her *telenovelas*." she said . "In fact, that's when she's the most dangerous,... so emotional,... powerful."

"I thought you didn't believe in *magica*."

"You don't listen well. It's because I'm a woman, isn't it?"

Hector smiled as if a secret had just been revealed and said, "Can't deny that."

"You must think I'm as stupid as you. Hell yes, I believe in *magica*. I just pretend not to. "

"If you believe in it, why don't you practice it?" said Hector. "It seems like it would be cool to have all that power."

"The *energia* is there for you too, but, because you're a man you're too stupid to know it."

"Don't call me stupid." Huevón said as he let her feel the back of his hand.

$$\therefore \Omega \therefore$$

A dreariness loomed over Lucha Obregon as she wheeled the baby *Jesus* in the recycled *gringo* stroller down to the *place of miracles*. Hardly a doting great-grandmother, she managed a degree of pleasure from pushing the child around the pier to watch the herons. The child always came alive as he watched the tall, long-legged birds poke around the shallows of Painted Pony Lake.

It was a bittersweet moment for Lucha to watch *Jesus* reach out at the herons and try to coax them over. She suppressed the inclination to teach him to reach out to the birds with the *energia*, to show him that the birds weren't really other than himself. But, *Jesus* Obregon was merely a boy and obviously lacked capacity, the illusion of separation that bewildered his mindstream would take several lifetimes to overcome, if the mindstream ever became aware of it. Lucha was convinced that the only option was to stand by and watch as *Jesus* floundered in the energy of his own grasping.

There always came a point when *Jesus* would become fed up with the birds ignoring him. He would throw something if he had something to throw. It was at these moments when Lucha came face to face with her grim situation and how far away she seemed from fulfilling her debt to the matrilineage.

And The Darkness Grasped It Not

1994
Waltonville, Aztlán

ENERGY FOLLOWS THOUGHT,
SACRED ENERGY FOLLOWS SACRED THOUGHT
--- SANG.GYES DO.RJE

Despite excruciating pain, Lucha Obregon managed to remain present during the birth of her baby, which was vital because Carmella Iroñia proved insufficient as a midwife. While Lucha tried to regain her breath between the contractive waves, she had to remind Carmella over and over of what was needed next in the birthing process. Angelica, very pregnant herself, could only look on in helpless admiration of her grandmother.

The emergence of the baby drew close and Lucha summoned the strength she had left. She closed her eyes and traced the symbols that conjure the *energia*. When the contraction finally came, she pushed until both shoulders finally cleared and the child came spilling out into this world. Lucha fought the urge to passout until she saw for herself that there was no penis.

"Nana, it's a girl." cried out Angélica.

The newborn was lifeless and didn't move in the slightest degree. Lucha feared that all had been for naught, that she had risked her life for nothing. Lucha raised her right hand slightly and scanned the lifeless infant. She could sense the life force within the child and engaged it with the intention of bringing about an increase. After a few moments, the infant gagged, coughed and then let out a welcome cry.

"See, I told you I could do it." said Carmella.

"What did you do?" said Angélica.

"Much more than you." said Carmella.

Lucha weakly reached out and said, "*Quietate*, the two of you and give me my daughter."

Carmella Iroñia wrapped the bloody, slick newborn in a small cotton wrap and placed it onto Lucha's chest. As she stepped back to let mother and child be with each other, Carmella saw that there was trouble.

"Lucha, you're bleeding."

"Probably just some tearing." said Angélica. "Remember Nana? I had that with *Chuy*."

"I don't think it's tearing. Look."said Carmella as she pointed toward Lucha's *puertá*.

An alarming stream of blood flowed from Lucha onto the bed. Carmella, inexperienced as she was with mid-wifery, wasn't prepared for something going wrong .

"Yarrow flowers. We need yarrow flowers. To stop the bleeding." said Carmella.

"Don't look at me. I don't know where they are." said Angélica. "You're the *pinche* midwife."

Carmella turned to Lucha and was stunned to see her calmly holding the infant, as though there wasn't a care in the world. As though nothing could spoil this moment between mother and daughter, *mujeres de Obregon*.

"I'll be right back with the flowers. Boil some water while I'm gone. At least you can be of some use." said Carmella as she hurried out of the house.

"Sit with us *m'hija*." said Lucha. "I don't think dried flowers are going to save me."

Angélica sat beside Lucha.

"Nana, I'm sorry I'm so useless."

"Hush now, *m'hija*, it's alright But, the time for that is over now. You're going to have to be her mother."

"What about this one inside of me?"

"Pray that she's healthy. Raise them both in the light of *magica divina*."

Angélica pressed a towel against Lucha, who was now bleeding more than ever as the placenta spilled out.

"Nana, why is this happening?"

"Let it happen *m'hija*. It's all part of it." said Lucha as she groaned.

Angélica reached out to take the infant from Lucha's chest, Lucha stopped her.

"Leave her with me until I'm gone." she said. "From then on she's your daughter, *m'hija*. Do you swear?"

"Of course, I do, Nana."

"Let me hear you say it, *m'hija*." said Lucha, growing weak.

"I swear Nana, I will raise her as my own daughter."

"So be it."

"Nana, I'm scared." said Angélica. "I don't know what I'm supposed to teach her. I squandered all my time with you."

"We all squander our time together, *m'hija*. We can only see it when it's too late to do anything about it."

"What am I supposed to do?"

"First you must settle down. Know that the *magica divina* is in your blood."

Lucha slowly held up her right palm toward Angélica and radiated *energia* into her aura, Angélica calmed profoundly, breathing deeply, slowly, rendered receptive.

"*M'hija*, first sit and find yourself in the stillness. Then dwell in the stillness until you know that you are not other than Goddess."

As she heard this, Angélica felt an intense shudder go down her spine. She felt the *energia* come from above her head down *sushumna* and come to rest in the *muladhara*. She experienced feelings that seemed outside of her body. The *energia* began to flow up her spine and out through the top of her head, she was suddenly aware that her consciousness was beyond her body, not seperate from it, but, no longer confined within it. Angelica shuddered deeply.

"After you discover that you are nothing other than Goddess, then live without hope and without fear. Let the Goddess-ness merge with the ocean of the infinite *magica divina*." said Lucha, fainter than before. "Now, bring me my *diario de sombre* and a paint brush. And bring the scepter. Hurry, *m'hija*."

Angélica needed a moment to come back in her flesh vehicle. When she was able to do so, she hurried off to collect the things her dying grandmother asked for. When she returned she found Lucha calmly caressing the infant girl.

"Give them to me. *m'hija*."

Aztlanicon

Lucha settled the infant on her belly so she could sit up ever so slightly. She opened the *diario de sombre* and dipped the brush into her magical puddles of blood on the bed.

"I empowered you when you were a little girl. But I never taught you the symbols."

As she grew weaker, Lucha painted the *magica divina* symbols. She taught Angélica as many of the 'words of power' as she could. It took several sheets of the shadow diary to paint them all.

For the first time in her life, Angélica Obregon had some clue of what her beautiful grandmother was talking about.

"When you're ready, you will find my journals, *m'hija*. Read them. They won't make sense to you at first. Don't stop, keep at it. Everything you need is in those journals."

Tears streamed from Angélica as she knew that the end was very near. Never had such love flown between them. Never had they been so close.

"*M'hija*, name them after your mother."

"Yes, Nana."

"Let me hear you say what you'll name them."

"Guadalupe and Evangelina." said Angélica.

"So be it".

"Nana, I'm sorry I fought you."

"Don't worry, *m'hija*. She who teaches learns. Be their teacher and you will learn."

Lucha reached beside her and handed the scepter of

the Obregon women to Angélica.

"Here *m'hija*, this is yours now. You now hold the matrilineage of *mujeres de Obregon.*"

It is not for human beings to know exactly when they've spoken their last words. Lucha Obregon had spoken hers. She slowly drifted back into the infinite field of all possibility, from which she had come.

Scepter of the Obregon Women

That Which The Eye Seeth Not

1994
Waltonville, Aztlán

9 HE CREATED HER IN THE HOLY GHOST, AND SAW HER, AND
NUMBERED HER, AND MEASURED HER.
--- ECCLESIASTICUS 1

When Carmella Iroñia returned with the dried yarrow flowers, it was immediately obvious that she was too late. Her designs on the matrilineage of *magica divina* were suddenly as lifeless as the death agony frozen in Lucha's face. Sitting on the bed with the tiny, magical child in her arms, Angélica Obregon gently swayed back and forth next to the bloody corpse. Carmella held out her arms as she slowly inched toward the bed.

"Don't worry. I'll take the child." she said.

Angélica turned away from her loudly.

"Nana made me swear to raise her as my own."

"You don't want to do this." said Carmella, as she moved closer.

"What are you saying? Nana's not even cold yet and you want me to go back on my word to her?"

"No one heard you make this promise. No one knows about this child."

"I know about her." said Angélica, as she gently caressed the slick, wrinkled newborn's skin. "I'm going to do what I promised Nana. I'm going to raise this girl like Nana wanted to raise me. I'm going to raise both girls in *magica divina*. As *mujeres de* Obregon."

"You were Lucha's only hope and you turned your back on her. You wanted nothing to do with *magica divina*."

"What do you know about it, *cuerva*? You don't have our blood." said Angélica defiantly.

"I know that when it meant the most, you chose to break her heart." said Carmella. "Now, when your *pinche* commitment means nothing, you're going through with it? This makes no sense."

"Don't you think I know it makes no sense?" said Angélica. "And no, it doesn't mean nothing. Now that Nana's dead, I can see that it means everything."

Carmella could tell that Angélica was committed for the moment, but how long would that last? She will surely be overwhelmed when her own infant is born in a few months. Then she will be nursing and caring for two infants, not to mention the male child *Jesus*, who still breastfeeds on occasion. There was no reason for Carmella to bring about a big battle over this now. She would be content to sit back and watch Angélica dine from a full plate of misery.

"I'll take care of the body then." said Carmella, changing the subject.

"How?"

"There are local people that do these things."

"You know such people?"

Carmella nodded slowly. "They'll make her death appear like domestic violence."

"How will they do that? No, don't tell me, I don't want to know."

"Her body will be found in one of the usual places, probably the *alcachofa* fields. The *gringo* authorities will come up with nothing. Just another dead illegal. Probably killed by a jealous husband or boyfriend. No big deal, happens every day around here. They'll give her an anonymous burial. Everyone will move on."

Angélica knew that the incompetent crone was right about making Lucha's corpse disappear. If the *gringos* found out about the baby, they'd take it away, maybe even take away the baby inside of her.

$$\therefore \, \Omega \, \therefore$$

As the three unsavory men from *La Tuberias* prepared to take the corpse away, Angélica was agitated by a feeling that something remained undone, but she had no inkling what it was.

She held the newborn child as she felt compelled to lean over and kiss the forehead of Lucha's corpse. A profound shiver went from the nape of Angélica's neck down her spine and then out her arms; both the child in her womb and the newborn in her arms kicked sharply at the same moment. Angélica had no idea what just happened, but things no longer felt undone.

Under the cover of darkness, the three men left with Lucha's corpse wrapped in a reflective silver tarp, they placed it in the trunk of a well restored '67 Chevy Impala. The Impala drove away into the grizzly night, no questions had been asked concerning the corpse's disposal. Angélica Obregon and Carmella Iroñia promised each other to keep the child's birth secret. Although she would never be forgotten, it was also agreed to not openly speak of Lucha again, at least, for the forseeable future.

Aztlanicon

∴ ♎ ∴

As she spent that entire fall in hiding with the baby girl, Angélica went through Lucha's belongings until she located the journals Lucha spoke of from her sudden deathbed. Just as Lucha said it would be, it was rough going for Angélica and she stumbled through the texts, at first. But with a degree of persistance that only women seem capable, Angélica waded through the journals until the truth contained within the visionary writings eventually guided her to the experience of the primordial state of being, where she discovered that she was nothing other than God, whatever that was.

Once this pivotal moment occured, Angélica began to perceive her grandmother's writings on the practice of *magica divina* in all their subtlety. Everything became shockingly easier and from then on Angélica pursued *magica divina* in earnest, with purpose and focus.

∴ ♎ ∴

The three months difference in their ages did nothing to diminish the perception that the Obregon girls were twins, not identical twins, but twins none the less; everyone thought so, even they thought so. When it came time to prepare a natal horoscope, Carmella Iroñia realized that the Sun had journeyed three signs of the zodiac between their births.

Clearly, the actual birthdates and times couldn't be used. That would obliterate the secret. Since there was no one to contradict the circumstances of the girl's nativity, Carmella settled upon using a date of birth exactly halfway between the two actual birth dates. That way the real horoscopes would be fused into one natal chart equally inaccurate toward each girl.

According to this fictitious natal chart, the twins were born when the Sun was in the sign of Scorpio, with Gemini being the sign on the rise. And so it was that the secret of the births was sealed and maintained. Because they shared a horoscope that didn't seem to apply to either of them, neither Guadalupe nor Evangelina would ever have much faith in astrology.

.˙. Ω .˙.

Over the course of several years, Angélica rose to the degree of *magica divina* she was capable, eventually to the level of Adept. When the twins reached the age of six, Angélica recognized that the occasion to pass along the *energia* lineage had arrived. She again read Lucha's shadowbook through and through, until she had internalized the teachings on initiation and felt confident enough to proceed. In quiet moments of repose, Angélica marveled at the wisdom of her deceased grandmother and the patience that never allowed her to give up on her wayward granddaughter.

Guadalupe, the elder twin, demonstrated an obvious magical capacity, but was not an authentic practitioner by any means. But, this *hechecera* training was somehow important to her mother, so she allowed the arcane knowledge to seep in a drop at a time until she became a puddle of knowledge within the vast ocean of *magica divina.*

Angélica was frustrated by Guadalupe's reluctance to take on the practice of the craft. *Magica* was of little use to Guadalupe, who was caught up in the glamour of the molecular world. The irony that a daughter of Lucha Obregon was resistant to *magica* made Angélica realize what she must have put Lucha through. On occasion Angélia couldn't help but dwell on how if she had just done what was asked of her, Lucha might still be alive.

Evangelina Obregon, the dark twin, was another matter entirely. Her interface with *magica divina* was inspired and she wielded it deftly, with little fanfare or public notice. Evangelina was content to exist in the shadows of this world. She, too, was beautiful, as all *mujeres de* Obregon are beautiful, but she didn't have the overarching need for attention, like her twin sister. Evangelina was satisfied to withhold her practice from the view of others. After all, she didn't want to end up like her mother's mother. Usually, instead of playing or gossiping with the other *chicas*, Evangelina was off by herself, her nose in some book or writing in her journal. Journals were a prominent trait of Obregon women, at least, most of them.

$$\therefore \; \Omega \; \therefore$$

It was well known thoughout the population of *La Madrecita* Parochial School, that Guadalupe Obregon and Lucy Baumbach disliked each other. Both were the *princesas* of their respective social circles. The two usually restricted their warfare to threatening glares across the wide cultural abyss that separated them.

Guadalupe was a *pochista,* ideally suited for *Aztlán*, as she was comfortable living between the two worlds of *la raza* and the *gringo*. Although the blood in her veins connected her body and spirit with the *magica divina*, Guadalupe was fascinated by the *gringo* world and acceptance into that world seemed agonizingly attainable. People found Guadalupe beautiful, magnetic and they simply wanted to be around her, this was true even among the *gringos*.

Hardly anyone wanted to be around Lucy Baumbach for any length of time. Lucy had magnetism, it was just the wrong polarity. But that didn't mean that the *gringo* children didn't gather around her. Lucy was from a prominent, powerful *gringo* family, after all. The children weren't stupid.

One Monday, during recess, Lucy Baumbach gathered her minions and quietly announced that a coven would be formed. Lucy had been to the movies over the weekend where she saw a film about four girls who get involved in magick. Their dalliance didn't end well for the girls in the movie, however, that fact somehow escaped Lucy's notice.

The thought of being witches and having magickal powers intriqued Lucy. It captured her imagination to the point that she made her mother take her to the bookstore, where she found a book on teenager witchcraft and made her mother buy it.

Over the course of that weekend Lucy consumed the text and experimented with the lessons until she became easily impressed with her new powers. Impressed to the degree that she decided upon forming a coven; of course, she'd be the leader. The nuns would never allow a coven within a parochial school, but that only made it all the more worth doing. Lucy decided upon the *façade* of a charity club. The nuns would fall for that. This coven idea also presented an opportunity to cut Guadalupe's power out from under her. Thus, Lucy's strategy would be to invite a chosen few of the *pochas*.

$$\therefore \, \Omega \, \therefore$$

Ordinarily, Guadalupe had little interest in whatever Lucy Baumbach was up to. But, when several from her circle were drawn over to the other side of the abyss, she thought it best to look into it.

"What are you guys doing with Lucy Baumbach?"

"We were invited to join their Youth Charity League." said Rita Calderon.

"Why would you want to join that?"

"You're just jealous because you weren't invited." said Hermosa Romero, who for the first time felt she had something over Guadalupe Obregon.

"What are you guys going to do in this Youth Charity League?"

"We're not supposed to talk about that with anyone outside the League. Sorry. We've got to go to a meeting."

Hermosa walked away in uncharacteristic exultation, the others followed with almost as much hurtful attitude.

Guadalupe had not known such deflation in her young life as when the four *pochas* walked over and joined the circle with Lucy and the *gringas*. There wasn't any real desire to go and be in their circle or to be in their *piche* Youth Charity League. The problem was that Guadalupe harbored a desperate loathing for exclusion from anything. A lack of interest in something was one thing; but, that wasn't the same as being excluded. The *princesa* knew it was inevitable that she would not only join the Youth Charity League, but take command of it.

∴ Ω ∴

After just a couple of meetings, rumors circulated around *La Madrecita* School that the Youth Charity League was secretly a witch coven aimed at domination of the school social scene. Upon hearing this, Guadalupe had new admiration for both the ingenuity and audacity of Lucy Baumbach. It was brilliant of her to conduct a coven right under the nose of Sister Monica, the *gringo* nun. Lucy would not be underestimated again.

Despite the new found admiration for Lucy's tactical prowess, Guadalupe also took notice of her errors in judgement. It was a mistake for Lucy to invite the *pochas* away from Guadalupe's circle. That alone begged a response from the *princesa* of the *pochas*. But, it was folly to invite Hermosa Romero into something that was supposed to be secret, that little *bicha* could never keep her mouth shut. Guadalupe knew that the ex-patriate *pochas* would be uncomfortable with the witchcraft aspect of the League. But the *ex-pochas* would continue to be involved with the *gringas* because of the obvious benefits that arise from hobnobbing with them.

Ordinarily, Guadalupe didn't want anyone knowing about her witchyness. Guadalupe was young and beautiful. There would be plenty of time for *magica* when she got old and lost her looks. But all of that seemed to change when she was excluded from the Youth Charity League.

The serpent-like nature of Guadalupe's competitiveness arose from slumber, ravenous for attention and restless to be unleashed. Once this ego-facet took command, Guadalupe would do anything to unseat Lucy Baumbach as the dominant witch at *La Madrecita* school. Finally, there was a practical use for all of the *hechecera* lessons that her mother put her through.

.˙. Ω .˙.

"Why do you care about this?" Evangelina said.

"I don't know. I just have to do it."

"It's because she took some of your *chicas*. Isn't it?"

Guadalupe didn't like it when her sister had that smile, it was almost always linked with something undeniable she had just said.

"Using the Craft to overthrow a school club? That's dumb." said Evangelina. "Stay out of it. Besides, you don't even use *magica*."

"I'm going to, as of now."

"What are you going to do?"

"I don't know, yet. It's got to be big though. So

everyone will see."

"Lupe, this is such a bad idea. Public displays are just what *hecheceras* don't need."

"What? It's bad to show them that I'm powerful?"

"Yes, exactly. It will make you a target."

"I'm doing it. You can act like my sister and help me or maybe you should go over and sit with Lucy Baumbach's Charity League.

"They already invited me. I said, no thanks."

"See what I mean? She insults me by inviting you and not inviting me."

"So what are you going to do?"

Guadalupe scanned the surrounding area and tried to imagine what she could do to show everyone her *magica*. Then she saw it.

"I'm going to bust up that thunderstorm coming this way."

Evangelina turned to the east, the direction her sister was pointing.

"That's too big for you to bust up. You don't practice enough."

"I bet I can do it if I'm skyclad."

"Skyclad is probably the only way you could do it and you're not going skyclad at school."

"Watch me."

Guadalupe rushed to the Music Room, where the choir robes were kept and then to the cafeteria for a handful of salt.

.˙. Ω .˙.

The other children gawked as Guadalupe, dressed in a choir robe, stepped onto the pitcher's mound and brought the softball game came to a rude halt. When she released the robe, it fell to the ground and she was revealed in all of God's glory. Too much of God's glory for some. There were gasps and there were catcalls and when she felt the attention of the entire playground focussed upon her, she faced the thunderhead that threatened from the east.

Guadalupe stood defiant before the oncoming storm and harnessed her intention. As she held aloft the handful of salt, she spoke the words of power. Winds began to whirl around her until a vortex formed and she became the center of the universe. She focussed the vortex *energia* into the handful of salt and cast it at the thunderhead while unleashing a sharp, loud yell. Immediately, the storm ripped apart down it's center, as if sliced by a titan's colossal sword. The clouds swirled away in mirror-imaged disruption and dissipated until the thunderstorm was no longer evident in the sky.

Guadalupe knelt down, picked up the robe and covered herself. She took a moment facing the east, she admired her handywork, imagining all the while that the Youth Charity League would walk over and beg her to be their leader.

Guadalupe turned back toward the other children, certain that the point had been made. She was staggered to see everyone glaring at her in horror. Everyone, except Sister Beryll, who had fainted to the ground. In that grim moment Guadalupe could sense the fear of the other children, fear that never manifested when she was content to be *princesa* of the *pochas*. But that time had now passed, a line had been crossed from which there was no return, at least at this school. Guadalupe turned and looked at her sister in dispair. Evangelina could only roll her eyes and shake her head.

$$\therefore \; \Omega \; \therefore$$

Sister Monica paced around her spartan office as Sister Beryll was sprawled on the small sofa, Sister Averell, the elder, was seated in the only chair. Sister Francis, the novice was off to the side, staying out of Sister Monica's way.

"No one is allowed to go near these girls. They are instruments of Evil." said Sister Monica.

"Can't we be more tolerant with them? They're just little girls. There was no harm done." said Sister Beryll through the damp towel over her face.

"No harm done? We had to pick you up off the ground." said Sister Monica. "It's up to us to weed out these disruptive influences among our students."

"Yes, but there are rumors that Lucy Baumbach's Charity League is actually a witch's coven. Won't we have to expel them also?"

"Those rumors are as yet unfounded. There is no proof that Lucy and those children in the Charity League are practicing witchcraft. There's no need to drag them into this."

"That might affect the large donations the Baumbach's make to the school." said Sister Averrel.

Sister Monica did not appreciate the irony intended by the elder nun's remark and let her know it with a glare.

"I was only mentioning it because our actions must be fiscally responsible. For the sake of the school." said Sister Averrel.

"Guadalupe Obregon proved herself a witch this afternoon. She can only blame herself for what is going to happen."

"But, Evangelina had nothing to do with this. Why are we expelling her?" said Sister Beryll.

"She can blame her sister for that. They came from the same womb. The same witch-mother. They have witch's blood and I want them out of here."

"Sister, you believe in witches?" said Sister Francis, the novice.

"Of course I do. The Lord believes in witches. Who are we not to?"

"Sister, how do we know that God believes in witches?" asked the novice.

" In the Book of Exodus, God said unto Moses, Thou shalt not allow a sorceress to live."

"So much for Thou shalt not kill." said Sister Beryll.

"Believe me, expulsion is much more lenient than what's described in scripture."

"Why doesn't scripture say anything about not allowing 'sorcerers' to live?" asked Sister Beryll.

"Sisters, I fear we're trifling with blasphemy here. That will be enough on this subject,... before one of you says something that cannot be taken back."

The nuns knew that Sister Monica was only speaking the current version of the truth. If God moved in mysterious ways, it only stood to reason that His Church would also. The nuns sat a few moments in silent bitterness, an acquired taste for that which comes with the calling.

∴ Ω ∴

So it was that Evangelina Obregon languished the rest of the day, while her show-off twin stormed about in the pungent air of the janitorial supply room; locked away from the other children. Foreverafter, both girls would be haunted by the smell of scented cleaning solvents.

The janitor stood up straight and grabbed at his keys when Sister Monica approached with Angélica Obregon.

"Why won't anyone tell me what's wrong?" asked Angélica. "Has something happened to my girls?"

"We had to isolate them from the other children."

"You've got them locked up?" said Angélica. "My babies?"

"They're a danger to the others. They're witches."

"How dare you say that to me."

"Where did they learn such things?" said Sister Monica with an accusing look.

Angélica said nothing, what was there to say?

"Regardless, these girls are not to come back to this school,... ever." said Sister Monica, as she turned to the janitor and pointed to the door.

The janitor pulled out his long key chain and thumbed through the keys until he found the right one and then leaned over and unlocked the door.

"Now take your witches away from here." said Sister Monica who then turned and walked away.

When the door is opened the two girls run to their

mother, who knelt down to embrace them.

"Mama, what did I do?" said Evangelina.

As she consoled the sobbing young girl, Angélica looked up at Sister Beryll with disgust. Sister Beryll averted her tearful eyes from the young mother and fought back her emotions.

"I hope that when the time comes, you all will be shown as much mercy as you have shown my girls." said Angélica Obregon.

$$\therefore \ \Omega \ \therefore$$

Angélica drove the broken-down old Mazda station wagon along Verdent Valley Road. The interior was as silent as it got in an old car. Guadalupe studied the water marks on the passenger window. Evangelina sat quietly in the back seat.

"I didn't know it was wrong." said Guadalupe.

"You didn't really do anything wrong, *m'hija*. At least not in the big picture."

"Then why did Sister Monica tell you never to bring us back there?"

Angélica didn't answer. Now was the dangerous time in her daughter's learning curve.

"Mama, they humiliate you for showing yourself. Why didn't you tell me?"

"I told you, but you never listen to me." said Evangelina.

Again, Angélica remained silent as she drove with her eyes blurred by the tears of tough love. She glanced in the rear view mirror and saw Evangelina in the backseat, her eyes magnified with fury.

"I'm never going to expose myself like that again." said Guadalupe, breaking the silence.

"Maybe that's best, for now, *m 'hija.*"

Evangelina resented that everything always had to be about Guadalupe. There was no discussion of her situation, which was entirely different. Here she was, cut off from her friends, if she actually had friends. But, if she did have friends she would be cut off from them solely for being Guadalupe's sister. She was fearful of what her life was to become. Silently, Evangelina made a vow of her own.

$$\therefore \; \Omega \; \therefore$$

Angélica thought it auspicious that the Sun was out on such a traumatic day as this. She brought her daughters often to the park at Painted Pony Lake, especially on days when the Sun was out. Painted Pony was a large pond more than a small lake, but it was peaceful; not only a sanctuary for the herons that wade its waters, but it also offered a brief asylum from the refugee way of life of the *Aztláno* people who lived in the Waltonville area.

But, more than any other reason, Angélica Obregon brought her daughters here to keep fresh their connection with the *Virgen de Guadalupe.* As they sat in what was left of the sunlight, Angélica reached into her purse and pulled out the small pouch made of blue brocade with gold accents. From the pouch she pulled out three mirrors and handed one each to Evangelina and Guadalupe. Evangelina immediately caught a sunbeam and carefully directed it onto the Holy Image. Angélica did the same. The three Obregon women, abominations in the eyes of the Church, sat in communion with their patron saint.

"Mama, should we be doing this? Didn't the *Virgen* kick us out too?" said Guadalupe. "Isn't she Catholic?"

"No, *m'hija*, she just pretends to be Catholic. It's because so many of her people are under the Church's thumb."

"So, now we're not under their thumb anymore?"

"I guess not." said Angélica.

Evangelina held the reflected sunbeam upon the image of the Aztlánicon and was absorbed in her connection with the energy of the *Vergen*.

"The *Virgen* still cares for us. She tells me not to worry. She will protect us no matter how stupidly Lupe behaves."

"Whatever." said Guadalupe. "I don't really need this tree to protect me. Besides, how much did it protect you today?"

"She says that your skepticism is healthy." said Evangelina.

"Good, I'm glad the tree approves."

There are many who consider such belief in the *Virgen* laughable. There are many who consider the notion of Aztlán laughable. For those few who require no molecular explanation, the image of the *Virgen* could only have been brought about by celestial genius unknowable to minds distracted by the conspiracy of the senses.

To Know The Creator,
Contemplate The Creature

1995
County Branciforte, Aztlan

35 TO ME BELONGETH VENGEANCE, AND RECOMPENCE;
THEIR FOOT SHALL SLIDE IN DUE TIME;
FOR THE DAY OF THEIR CALAMITY IS AT HAND,
AND THE THINGS THAT SHALL COME UPON THEM
MAKE HASTE.

--- DEUTERONOMY 32:

A secret meeting was sought by the *Culto Sabidurias*, a dominant *familia* of the era. It had to be like the meeting never took place, so no one would accuse them of seeking the counsel of a woman. That would show a weakness that no one could afford to display. This secret meeting was to take place on the westside of the coast highway, at the roadside rest area between Waltonville and the exit for De Selvia Beach. It was a great place to watch the sunset, but, hardly anyone did that.

Mostly the rest area was frequented by travelers desperately needing to pee or promiscuous *gringos* having reckless, clandestine sex. It was a great place to have a meeting without being noticed.

As the sun was going down, the *Culto* drove up in their hyper-restored Impala. *Doña* Salamanca and her two sons had no choice but to turn their backs on the magnificent sunset. The dark beauty told Nestor and Eberto to stay back as she cautiously approached the passenger side. As the *Doña* paused to admire the car's condition, the window rolled down and out peeked *Don* Antonin Zopenco.

"What year is this? Sixty-six?" she said.

"Sixty-seven. I wanted a sixty-six, but couldn't find one."

"Very nice, just the same."

The rear door swung open and a sizable minion stepped out. He nodded graciously and opened the passenger door. The *Don* slowly, gingerly got out of the car.

"Thank you for meeting with me. I wasn't sure if you'd actually go through with it."

She was unsettled by his middle-aged-ness and wondered if time had been so brutish to herself.

"You look good. It's been a long time."

"I could say the same, but I'm not going to lie to you."

Don Zopenco absorbed the barb and shuffled around for another subject. He looked over at the two vigilant young men who seemed ready to pounce if there was any attempt to harm their mother.

"They look like their fathers." said the *Don*.

"What do you want, Antonin?"

"Do they know?"

"Everyone who knows is either dead or standing here looking at each other. I want it kept that way."

"How do you intend to keep such a big secret? He looks nothing like Salamanca. He does look like you though."

"I'll do what I have to do. Now what do you want?"

"Don't you think they should know? For no other reason than the disposition of your *familia* if something should happen to you."

"You mean if you kill me like you had my husband killed?"

Nestor and Eberto reached for their guns as they moved swiftly toward their mother. The *Doña* put up her hand to calm them, she put up the other to calm the *Don's* minion.

"I had nothing to do with Salamanca's death. I swear it upon my thumbs that hang in your *hacienda*." said Zopenco, holding up his hands to show his prosthetic thumbs.

She looked surprised.

"You didn't think I knew did you?"

"No."

"We've all lost something along the way, *Doña* Salamanca."

The *Doña* stiffled her urge to snicker at seeing Zopenco's missing thumbs. In a very real sense, they caused Emiliano to live on for her. Even dead, he could make her laugh.

"So you heard about what happened at the lake?" said Zopenco.

"*Si.*"

"They say she used to work for you until she had some vision of the *Virgen*."

"It's like I've said all along." said Rosalie. "Don't underestimate the bother caused by a virgin.."

"Well, you've probably heard that the *movemiento*

revolutionario has declared the site as 'ground zero' of Aztlán."

"I'm sure the *gringos* are devastated to hear it. They'll be fleeing their precious California by the millions."

"While you bring in migrants by the thousands."

"How else are you going to fight your revolution if we don't import soldiers."

"That's what we want to talk to you about. Being a *coyote* is no life for a beautiful woman like you."

"So it would be more appropriate if I was less good looking? This is the last time I'm going to ask. What do you want Zopenco?"

"We want to take over your *familia*."

"Fuck this."said *Doña* Salamanca as she turned and walked toward her car.

Zopenco called out, "You always were such a hard ass, Rosalie."

While Eberto opened the rear passenger door for her, Zopenco decided to take a parting shot.

"Why don't you tell him who his father really was."

The *Doña* turned and gave a glare that bordered on criminal behavior. Zopenco would have never allowed such a gesture to go unpunished if she were a man, instead he simply stood there as the Lincoln towncar drove away.

∴·᎒᎒﹏᎒﹏᎒᎒∴·

Thou Shalt Bring Forth Many Branches

᎒᎒﹏᎒﹏᎒᎒

1968
Encarnation College
Waltonville, California

To the *gringo* authorities, *familia Salamanca* held a prominent position in the human smuggling trade of the southwest United States, the region that would come to be known as *Aztlán*. The lore of *la familia* centers around a tragic, young couple, as mismatched as they come. Rosalie Sandoval and Emiliano Salamanca found each other during the tumultuous 60's. They attended the same college, but for entirely different reasons.

Rosalie Sandoval was the youngest daughter of the only *Hispanic* rancher in the Branciforte valley. Raised in the ancient *hacienda* on the Sandoval *rancho,* Rosalie was to inherit the Mexican land grant that had domiciled the Sandoval name since before the *gringo* conquests. As she emerged from the counselor's office in the college administration building, she paused for a moment and walked up to the only person in sight.

Emiliano Salamanca, an heir to nothing, leaned back against a fake *adobe* wall and invented answers to questions that had not yet been posed. He was so lost inventing, he didn't even notice her walk up.

"She said to send in the next person. Is that you?"

Emiliano looked up as though interrupted from something crucial. Suddenly, he was caught in her eyes. Just like that, the vector of his life was altered. Nothing would ever be the same.

Aztlánicon
Thou Shalt Bring Forth Many Branches

"You can go in now." she said and turned away.

He watched her as she walked down the hall, she carried herself with purpose and expectation, serious on so many levels. She was way out of his league, but, that feeling she brought out of him was compelling. As she walked away, she gave a little glance back at him. He was tempted to call out to her, to plead with her to bring it all back.

"Mr. Salamanca, are you coming in?" said the voice from the office behind him.

Upon entering the threshold, Emiliano discovered a handsome black woman with her hair piled up high, like an African mushroom cloud. Around her neck she wore a pewter *Ankh*, because it was groovy to do so. In her hand she held up a manilla folder, his folder.

"Congratulations, Mr. Salamanca. You have one of the most unremarkable transcripts I've ever seen." she said.

"Thank you, I guess."

"Do you have any idea why I've asked for this meeting?"

"To congratulate me?"

She paused with a smile.

"No. We have a problem, Mr. Salamanca."

"What's that?"

"You've spent the last three semesters floundering around, all helter skelter, in survey courses. Intro to autoshop, intro to home economics, criminal justice. In which you got an incomplete."

"I've still got to finish the term paper."

She looked at him suspiciously.

"Alright, I've got to start the term paper."

"Your student deferrment is hanging by a thread. If you haven't accomplished significant work towards a declared major by the end of next semester, the school is required to inform the draft board. It's that simple."

Emiliano tried to conceal the wince from her. As was his habit, he glanced away in the hope that life's venom might dilute just a little. It didn't. Slowly, Emiliano lifted his eyes upon her and mingled with her energy.

"Look, if I'm drafted, they're going to send me over to Vietnam, or Laos or wherever they are now."

"So then, you're only going to college to stay out of the Army?"

"And the Navy and the Marines. I want to stay out of all that shit."

The counselor failed to conceal her amusement, "I'd keep that to myself if I were you Mr. Salamanca."

"Why? Did I say something wrong?"

"That sort of attitude is frowned upon. We want serious students here at Encarnacion."

"I'm as serious as it gets about staying out of the draft."

"Don't you want to serve your country?"

He looked askance, "I'm the bastard child of migrant farm laborers. At what moment did this become my country?"

Again, she smiled, "Let's see if we can't find you a major." She scanned his records. "So there's no course of study that interests you?"

"Not really. Academics was never my strong point."

"Well, I suggest you work on making them your strong point, Mr. Salamanca. Especially, if you want to stay in college and out of the draft."

"You'd be the same way if you were in danger of getting drafted. If they drafted women."

"If they drafted women? I certainly wouldn't be squandering my time like you seem to be doing. And you'll probably still end up getting drafted."

"Don't say that. I don't need to go over there to get shot at. There's plenty of people around here who want to shoot at me. We need to deal with that."

"Now you sound like the MOFA people."she said.

"Who?"

"You took "Intro to Chicano Studies" and you never heard of MOFA?"

"No, never heard of it."

"It's a *chicano* organization here on campus. They're on college campuses all over. I'm shocked that you've never heard of it before. That young woman that was just in here. She's the president of the campus chapter."

Emiliano could still smell her, still feel her presence, still see her face.

"I'm afraid I've never met her."

"Rosalie Sandoval is her name. She's one of the top students in the *Chicano* Studies. She also TA's for Rudolpho Aguirre."

"Theee ... Rudolpho Aguirre?"

"Yes, the famous Rudolpho Aguirre."

"She works for him?"

"She's a TA, teacher's aid. You have no idea of what goes on at this college, do you?"

"No, not really."

"Since you don't have any plans beyond carrying twelve units, why don't we declare your major in *chicano* studies?

"I don't know about that."

"Come on, you're *chicano*, how hard could it be? We'll get you started on some of the required courses and then we won't have to inform the draft-board of anything. How's that sound?"

"That part sounds pretty good,"

As the counselor filled in the forms, Emiliano was overcome by that feeling you get when you realize the car you just bought is a lemon.

$$\therefore \Omega \therefore$$

The familiar energy of humiliation percolated in Emiliano's neck, just beneath his ears, as he squirmed in the back row of the lecture hall during his torturous first few days as a *Chicano* Studies major.

Adrift in his pudgy, mid-life years, Rudolpho Aguirre, a folkhero of the coming *revolucion,* paced around the lectern in his usual widdershim manner. Aguirre was grilling the unfortunate Emiliano over information that he obviously didn't bring with him.

"Again you attend my class unprepared, Salamanca. Why do you bother with showing up for the abuse you know that I'm going to give you?"said Aguirre."Haven't you read the text?

"He probably can't even afford the text, professor." said Antonin Zopenco, the leader of the social group known as the *Vigilantes*.

As the chuckles scattered throughout the lecture hall, Emiliano merely sat in his puddle of shame. Rosalie Sandoval wasn't laughing, though. Instead, she looked at him like he was a drowning puppy or a greeting card kitten hanging by one paw.

"Let me assure you Mr. Salamanca. Let me assure all of you,... no one will survive *Chicano* Studies just because they think they're *Chicano*."

Like a dog in the presence of a powerful shaman, Emiliano looked away, hoping to lessen the sting, it didn't.

"It's lucky for you we don't have the time today to make a real example out of you. Next week we'll cover chapter seven of the text, "The Rise and Fall of the Aztecs. Salamanca, see that you're prepared for once."

Rudolpho Aguirre packed his books and papers into his tooled Mexican leather briefcase and promptly left the lecture hall. Emiliano waited for everyone else to exit before he even looked up. As he scooted down the aisle, he saw that Rosalie Sandoval waited for him.

"He was rough on you."

"Yeah."

"Fuck him."

Emiliano slowly smiled.

"You know you're way behind the class, but I can help you catch up if you want." said Rosalie.

"I would like that very much. As you can tell, I could really use the help." he said. "The only thing is that I can't afford to pay you. That guy was right. I can't even buy the text. It was either that or the electricity bill."

"Don't worry about that. We'll figure something out. You have to catch up with the class first." she said. She handed her copy of the textbook to him."Read the chapter on the "Rise and Fall of the Aztecs.""

Emiliano accepted the book , "Don't you need this?"

"I can spare it for a weekend. I've read it already."

"Of course you have."

"I don't need it back until Monday. Meet me under the *encina* grove around ten thirty."

Again, Emiliano found himself watching Rosalie Sandoval walk away, his eyes were trained on her as she disappeared through the door. It was then that Emiliano noticed Antonin Zopenco eyeballing him. Obviously Zopenco didn't like something, perhaps he wanted Rosalie for himself. Why wouldn't he? Everyone wanted her. But, if the brightest and most beautiful student in the department was offering help, Emiliano was not going to refuse it. If that made Zopenco his enemy, so be it.

$$\therefore \Omega \therefore$$

On a blanket made damp by mid-morning fog, Rosalie and Emiliano studied in the *encina* grove on that following Monday. Emiliano ceased his cramming and looked up at her.

"Why do you help me?"

"What?" she said, annoyed by the interruption.

"Why do you help me?"

Thou Shalt Bring Forth Many Branches

"I don't like to stand by and do nothing while a helpless creature is being tortured. I'm just not that kind of person."

"Thanks alot. Is that what you think, I'm a helpless creature?"

"You're not helpless. I'm helping you." She gave him the slightest of smiles.

"Look you're the best student in the department. Everyone here would love to have you tutor them. Even Aguirre himself."

She looked at him and closed her book.

"You're right. What am I doing wasting time with a *nadie* like you?" she said. "I could be spending quality time with that chubby brown asshole."

"You're not one of those that wonder what it would be like to sleep with a folkhero?"

"Maybe when he was younger and in better shape. Now, it would probably be like having sex with a bowl of tepid *flan*."

"Tepid?"

"Lukewarm."

They both cringed at the thought.

"What do you really think about all of this Aztlán business?"

"Like most social movements, it's a joke." she said.

"A joke? How can you say that? You're the president of the MOFA chapter."

"If the future of Aztlán depends on the likes of self-centered *culos* like Rudolpho Aguirre or Antonin Zopenco, then I think we shouldn't even bother."

"You're talking about the chair of the *Chicano* Studies department."

"I know who I'm talking about."

"Why do you say that?"

"Because of this *chicano* boycott they want to put in *El Plan de Aztlán*."

"What's that?"

"What's a boycott?"

"No, what's *El Plan de Aztlán*?"

"God, you really don't know shit, do you?"

"I'm moldable. Mold me."

It occured to Rosalie in that moment that molding this young man into something useful could be a worthwhile undertaking.

"*El Plan de Aztlán* It's like a declaration of independence. It's going to be unveiled at the MOFA congress this coming March in Denver."

"Are you going to that?"

"Yes I am. There's three delegates going. I'm one. Zopenco is another. The third hasn't been elected yet."

"I'm going to be that third one."

She looked at him askance. "You've got alot of catching up to do before Aguirre is going to let that happen."

"What's he got to do with it?"

"He's the faculty advisor. The bylaws say that the faculty advisor appoints the delegates, but Aguirre decided to hold an election for the third spot."

"Man of the people stuff."

"Exactly."

"So then, he has a lot to do with it. I have to work on that. Now what about this boycott?"

"It's a boycott by *chicano* students until the entire educational system is revamped into a level playing field."

"How likely is it to happen?"

"Not very likely they're going to revamp the educational system because of a few upset *chicano* students." she said.

"No, I mean how likely is this boycott?"

"If Aguirre and the rest of the hot-heads have their way, it'll happen next September."

"I can't be a part of any damned boycott. They're telling me that my student deferrment is hanging by a thread as it is. Is this a done deal?"

"Not if we can keep that section of the document from being adopted."

"Now I have to become a delegate. To prevent this *pinche* boycott."

Y ou should also take notes for the term paper that's due at the end of next week." said Rosalie.

"Oh shit, I forgot about that."

"Have you even chosen a topic?"

"Not really." said Emiliano, he noticed her incredulous look. "I'm kind of famous for being late on term papers."

"If you want to go as a delegate to this congress, you'd better turn in a hell of a term paper."

"I don't have a typewriter."

"They have a bunch of them at the library. Do you type?" said Rosalie.

"I hunt and peck. It takes me about a day and a half to get a full page with no typos."

"Look, I won't write the paper for you, but I will help you with it. At least I can type it for you."

She handed over a piece of blank paper.

"Here, write something. Let's see if I can read your handwriting."

Emiliano took out his pen, wrote on the paper and showed it to her.

You're an angel.

"Let's see if you still feel that way after you've worked with me for awhile."

$$\therefore \Omega \therefore$$

Emiliano entered the lecture hall and felt their eyes trained on him, there was more than the usual din. He walked to the steps, slinked past Rosalie seated in the designated TA seat, about where the 'first violin' would sit in an orchestra. Rosalie urged him to be strong with a subtle look and a clinched fist. As Emiliano climbed the steps, one of the already seated students called out.

Aztlánicon
Thou Shalt Bring Forth Many Branches

"Hey, new guy, since you showed up, Aguirre hasn't messed with me even once. Thanks."

There was clapping and whooping.

"Glad I could help." Emiliano said, as he bowed to his dubious admirers.

He climbed the steps to a row of empty seats way up top in the lecture hall and turned to face the music. Things quieted down considerably when Rudolpho Aguirre entered. Even though the conversations ended abruptly, the students turned toward their professor with new found confidence. It was fully expected that Aguirre would pickup where he left off, smacking around the new punching bag. It was the common opinion that all the class had to do was sit back and watch without showing too much delight in the new guy's torture.

Even though Rudolpho Aguirre was a noted writer of *latino* subject matter, his folkhero status among California *chicanos* was earned for being the right hand of the great Alphonse Guarango in the final, potent years of the Great One's life, when no one knew they were the final, potent years.

Aguirre was credited with organizing the famous Delano boycott, the first victory for the farm labor movement in Califas, which was how California was known among the *Chicanos*. The *huelga* was long and costly, but did result in improved working conditions for a time, at least, until the murder of Alphonse Guarango. In the chaos that followed the assassination, the energy of the boycott entropied and the relentless farmers re-built their *reich* stronger than ever.

With the great man gone, there was no coin to glean in his wake. The bottom fell out of the revolution industry for Rudolpho Aguirre and he needed a soft place to land. When he learned of the creation of a *chicano* studies department at Encarnacion College, he pushed hard for a teaching position. Getting the position was not easy.

Even though Aguirre was published, the two books he'd written were not scholarly works. But, in the end Alphonse Guarango left behind a residue of credibility that had brushed off on Aguirre and that was enough to seize the day. Even in death, Alphonse Gaurango continued to be of use for Aguirre.

"Alright people, let's get started. The rise and fall of the Aztecs. Let's see what you've gotten from the text."

Emiliano winced as he could already imagine the sound of his name filling the room. He was not let down.

"Mr. Salamanca."

The anticipation within the lecture room was palpable. Emiliano could feel the collective glare of the other students trained upon him.

"Good morning, sir." said Emiliano.

"What caused the power vacuum of the eleventh and twelfth centuries in central Mexico?"

"The fall of the Toltecs."

Aguirre was stunned at the promptness and relevance of Emiliano's response.

"That was obviously too easy. What group emerged to fill that vacuum?"

"The Culhuacáns, who later evolved into the Aztecs."

Professor Aguirre glared at Rosalie, he knew full well that this was her doing. She'd obviously taken pity on this fool with the intention of depriving her Professor of the opportunity to torture him publicly.

"Very good. Let's move on." Aguirre glared at the seating chart. Concern spread through the entire lecture hall, many squirmed in the knowledge that, like a heat-seeking missile that had lost it's target, Aguirre would now have to acquire another.

Just as Rosalie expected, Emiliano's sudden competence let the air out of Aguirre's balloon. What she didn't expect was for Emiliano to put his hand up in order to take the cruel spotlight back upon himself.

"Professor, could I ask a question?"

A collective sigh of relief filled the hall; even Aguirre relaxed.

"Yes, what's your question?"

"Sir, this chapter presents this idea of a power vacuum."

"Yes? What about it?"

"The concept of a power vacuum implies that it's the natural condition of things for someone to be in power. Like there's some kind of imbalance if no one is lording over someone else."

"I don't see what you're getting at. All civilized people accept the need for governance."

"Doesn't it all depend on perspective? From the point of view of the Nazi's, wouldn't they see the same condition as a facism vacuum?" Wouldn't the time period of this vacuum, wouldn't that pretty much fit the definition of paradise?"

"How so?"

"As far as *la raza* is concerned, isn't a power vacuum exactly what we want? Doesn't freedom only exist in a power vacuum? No one is being domineered by anyone else."

"In other words, you're suggesting there be no civilization as we know it." Aguirre said in a way that invited the class to snicker.

With strategic respect Emiliano said, "Yes sir."

"Class, I believe we have an anarchist in our midst."

The class relaxed; Rudolpho Aguirre took his coffee cup from the desk and slowly sipped while he thought about what he was going to do with this gift.

"I've never thought of it. But, when you put it like that, I suppose I am an anarchist."said Salamanca.

Rosalie braced for what might be about to happen. She looked at Emiliano. He could tell that she thought he was nuts. Antonin Zopenco observed the glance between the two.

Aguirre took one last sip, set the cup down and resumed his slow widdershim path around the lectern.

"Mr. Salamanca, don't you think history has shown over and over that there is a social class that should be in charge of things?"

"I think there is a class of people that think they should be in charge of things and that's the problem. We'd be better off without people that think that way."

"So, you're suggesting what? That we live in chaos? Without any social order?"

"I don't see how it could be much worse than what we have now, sir."

"The revolution is going to fix what's wrong." said Antonin Zopenco. "Once *la raza* is in control, everything that's wrong is eventually going to be made right."

"There you have it, Mr. Salamanca,"said Aguirre. "*La gente* believes the revolution will fix these things.".

"If revolutions fixed anything, Professor, then why

do we have to keep having them?" said Emiliano.

Tense laughter gnawed at the hall's thick atmosphere.

"So then, you're not in favor of the *revolucion*? You want to leave *la raza's* homeland occupied and controlled by the *gringo?*" said Aguirre.

"I guess that brings us back to my question about your power vacuum. If the *revolucion* simply means some other elitists are waiting in the wings to takeover control, then as far as *la gente* are concerned, what difference does it make?"

"I'll tell you what difference it makes,"said Zopenco. "*La gente* would rather be under the control of *chicanos* than *gringos.*".

"Spoken like a true elitist." said Emiliano. "If that's true, why do so many people leave Mexico to come up here to escape the control of *chicano* elitists? Isn't Mexico under the control of *chicanos?*"

"No, Mexico is under the control of Europeans." said Aguirre.

If that's the way you feel, why are you in *chicano* studies?" said Zopenco.

"They said I have to have a major to maintain my student deferment."

At that moment Rosalie Sandoval wondered what the hell Emiliano was thinking. By exposing himself that much, Aguirre was sure to crush him publicly. She looked at Emiliano to signal to him to shut up.

Professor Aguirre stood silent for the moment until he decided on his next move. He reached out, gathered his papers and put them in his briefcase.

"Alright, that's enough for today. Class is dismissed."

The students were let down that there wasn't more to witness, they gathered their belongings and began to file out of the hall.

"Mr. Salamanca, Mr. Zopenco and Ms. Sandoval. I'd like to speak with the three of you." said Aguirre.

The three of them sat in the front row. When everyone else was gone, Aguirre turned to them.

"I've decided that the three of you will be our delegation to the MOFA Congress."

The three looked at each other, not sure how to react.

"Professor, of course I'm going, that's a given." said Zopenco. "And, I guess there's a case to be made for sending the *chica*, but Salamanca is a traitor to *la causa*. Not to mention, he's a nobody."

"You're all nobodies." said Aguirre. "Any credibility this delegation has comes from me. Remember that."

"Professor, I have to object here." said Zopenco. "The MOFA chapter was preparing to have an election."

"The rules clearly state that the delegation will be appointed by the faculty advisor." said Aguirre. "Are you the faculty advisor, Zopenco?"

There was no response.

"Sir," said Emiliano, "I can see why you want Zopenco and Ms. Sandoval, but, why me? I thought you disagreed with what I was just saying."

"Obviously, you're controllable. You respond well to tutelage." said Aguirre. "You'll be useful to my delegation."

"Sir, just so you understand that I'm against this student boycott." said Emiliano. "I can't vote in favor of that."

"Salamanca, it makes no difference to me what you're against?" said Aguirre. "You'll vote how I tell you to vote."

Suddenly, Emiliano was overcome with clarity of how screwed he was.

"Wouldn't our delegation be more credible if it was elected?" said Zopenco.

"Why? What credibility is there in being elected by a bunch of know-nothing students?" said Aguirre.

"Any delegation sent by the great Rudolpho Aguirre has to have credibility within *la camara*." said Rosalie. "And that's the problem."

"She speaks, at long last." said Aguirre. "Don't you have anything to add to this discussion, Ms. Sandoval? Seeing as how you are the delegation's biggest problem."

Emiliano jumped back into it, "Why is she the biggest problem? She's the best student."

"Precisely. And she's the most qualified to lead the delegation." said Aguirre.

"So why is she the problem?" said Emiliano.

Professor Aguirre looked at Rosalie to see if she wanted to answer the question.

"Because, I'm a woman." said Rosalie.

"No shit because you're a woman." said Zopenco.

"Sir, I hate to admit it, but Zopenco has a point." said Rosalie. "How would you explain not having an election? We've promoted it for weeks."

Emiliano was taken by Rosalie's ease in moving on from an insult, even he felt more insulted than she appeared.

"Don't worry *niños*, you'll have your *pinche* election." said Aguirre. "Salamanca will be on the ballot with all of the others. I'll be in charge of counting the votes and announcing the results. As far as everyone is concerned, democracy will have been served."

"So this is how it will work." said Zopenco. "I'll be the leader, the *chica* will be the follower. Salamanca will watch as the alternate."

"As usual, Mr. Zopenco, you misinterpret the situation." said Aguirre, he addressed Rosalie directly. "You've been my greatest hope these past few years, but I've never seen a way around your unfortunate birth,... until today. No, Mr. Zopenco, you'll be the one watching as the alternate. Good day, everyone."

Professor Aguirre gathered his briefcase and walked toward the door, Zopenco followed closely behind to plead his case.

Emiliano called out, "Why are you so sure that I'll do what you want? How do you know that I'll even go to Denver?"

"You'll either go to Denver or you'll go to VietNam. It's your choice, Mr. Salamanca." said Aguirre as he exited the hall with Zopenco in tow.

Aztlánicon:
A Dangerous Precipice Of Vanity

∴·⁹⤙)Ω(⤚ᶜ·∴

A Dangerous Precipice Of Vanity

⁹⤙⤙⤚⤚ᶜ

March, 1969
Denver, Colorado

Later, on the first day of the *congreso*, Emiliano returned to the afternoon meeting of *la camara,* at a secret off-campus location. These all important drafting meetings were being held off-campus to allow the *congreso* to put together their revolutionary document, *El Plan Espiritual de Aztlán*, while still preserving the facade of an innocuous *chicano* cultural festival on campus. This deception was critical to manuevering the school administration into allowing any sort of *chicano* gathering. A *chicano* cultural festival proved to be under everyone's radar.

As Emiliano squeezed into the standing room only gathering, he could hear the piercing voice of that *putapocho*, Luiz Vargas, reading aloud the current draft of the secret document.

"The front line defense will come from the *barrios,* the *campos*, the *pueblos*, and the *ranchitos*." said Vargas. "Their involvement as protectors of their people will be given respect and dignity. Those who place themselves in the front ranks for their people do so out of love and *carnalismo*."

"*Carnalismo?*" said Emiliano from the back of the room, loud enough for everyone to hear. "Luiz Vargas dares to utter the word *carnalismo?*"

Vargas rolled his eyes, "Great, he's back."

"Mr. Vargas, since you're the least brotherhood oriented person imaginable? Would you please define *carnalismo* for the rest of us. Just so we know what the hell you're talking about."

All through the morning session, Emiliano and Luiz Vargas butted heads over what was intended for the final draft of the document. Sadly, it seemed obvious to everyone in the room that the afternoon session would be no less tedious.

El Plan de Aztlan was the brainchild of a certain conclave of MOFA members that gathered the previous August in Isla Vista. This conclave was composed of the *chicano* studies departments from campuses all over Califas. Antonin Zopenco represented MOFA de Encarnacion. Luiz Vargas was the alpha-male of the *chicano* student population at Don Diego College.

Vargas and his *utopianistas* spent weeks preparing their draft of the document and they presumed it would simply be read, lavishly praised and ratified without contention. None of them was prepared for this nobody from northern Califas to force them to trudge through the document line by line, to justify every damned sentence. This bullshit was unacceptable to the *utopianistas*.

To allow delegates from different MOFA chapters to get to know one another, there was a bar-b-que following the close of business that first day of *la camara*. Rosalie was attending the official on-campus gathering for the presidents of the various MOFA chapters. These gatherings were critical to the success of the *congreso* and were a great sacrifice made by the various chapter presidents. Their involvement in the '*chicano* cultural festival' meant that they would not attend the secret meetings of *la camara*, where the real work of the *chicano congreso* was being accomplished.

So, Emiliano attended the bar-b-que alone, while Antonin Zopenco was with other *utopianistas*.

"It makes you wonder what Rudolpho Aguirre is up

to, sending someone like that." said Luiz Vargas.

"I told you this asshole Salamanca is a traitor to *la causa*." said Antonin Zopenco.

"Can't you talk some sense into him?" said Vargas.

"I'm only the alternate."

"What the hell is going on up there at Encarnacion? What kind of MOFA chapter are you guys running?" said Vargas.

"It's all fucked up. We've even got a *chica* president."

Having made no fans that day, Emiliano sat alone at the bar-b-que and thought nothing of it when a beautiful young *chicana* approached him carrying two plates of food.

"Have you eaten yet?" she said.

"No."

"Would you like to eat with me?"

Emiliano smiled, took the plate and offered her a seat at the folding card table.

"Hi, I'm Hilda and you're Emiliano, right?"

"Yeah. How did you know that?"

"Oh, I asked about you."

"Who?"

"I forget their name." she said, changing the subject. "So, are you enjoying things so far?"

"I guess." he said. "Where do you go to school?"

"Don Diego State."

"With Luiz Vargas?"

"Yeah, he's not such a bad guy, when you get to know him."

"I take that to mean that you've gotten to know him?"

She glared at him, but then drifted back as though nothing had been said.

"You were giving him a pretty hard time in there today." she said.

"It wasn't anything personal. It's just that this document is very important."

"No shit. There's been a lot of time and energy put into it already."

"So the rest of us aren't supposed have anything to say about it? We're just supposed to accept it as is?"

"Well, yeah. We *chicanos* have to stick together, right?"

Emiliano looked at her in disbelief, "I'm sorry but I just can't do that. I can't just not say anything about things I strongly disagree with."

"That's what we thought." she said. "I guess we'll have to agree to disagree. *Manga*,... your food is getting cold."

$$\therefore \Omega \therefore$$

Two days later, even at death's door, flat on his back in the *pinche* motel room, Emiliano continued to jump through hoops for the *Man*. Worn down by a gastro-intestinal system run amok, not to mention near lethal headaches, he laid weak and empty on the dilapidated bed,

Aztlánicon:
A Dangerous Precipice Of Vanity

wondering how he could salvage the mission forced upon him by Rudolpho Aguirre. There was a knock at the door.

"No housekeeping." he yelled, then grabbed the sides of his head in anguish.

Again, there is a knock. Emiliano slowly sat up and took a deep breath, he exhaled and allowed his energy to settle before he got up and opened the door.

"What's happened to you? You've missed most of it. Zopenco has taken over our delegation." said Rosalie. "Where have you been?"

"Traveling between the bed and the toilet mostly." he said.

"Are you alright?"

"Yeah, I think the worst of it's over. So have I really missed it? How long have I been out of it?"

"There's one last meeting of *la camara* this afternoon and then the final ceremony this evening. Maybe you should clean yourself up and then get some rest."

∴ Ω ∴

When Rosalie woke up, she'd been asleep against his chest, so glad that she had him take a shower and brush his teeth. She got up and crossed the room, over to the window. She pulled aside the thick drapes enough to cover her nakedness. She leaned over and peered outside, the sun was low in the sky.

Emiliano rustled in the bed, she turned to see him propped up on his elbows.

"Since we're in Denver. Does that mean we're in the mile high club now?" he said.

"I don't know for certain, but I think being in an airplane might be mandatory?"

"Exhausted sex is the best." he said.

"Don't you mean exhaust-ing sex?"

"No, I said what I meant. If you're not satisfied, give me a chance to make it up to you." he said as he patted the mattress.

"We don't have time for that now. Remember? Student deferrment hanging by a thread? Take another shower and get dressed."

He knew that she was right, they had to get to the conference finale. He slid out of the bed and went into the bathroom. He poked his head out slightly to sneak another peek at her naked. For the first time, he saw the tattoo on the small of her back.

GUTTA CAVAT LAPIDEM
NON VI,
SED SAEPE CADENDO

"What's that above your ass?" he said.

She turned toward him, "A tattoo. I thought you were taking a shower."

"I know it's a tattoo. But, what's it mean?"

"It's an old axiom in Latin."

"What's an axiom?" he said.

"Go look it up."

"Look it up? Come on. Why are you being so mean? Just tell me." he said.

"I'm not being mean, I'm being strong for your sake. How do you think I found out what it meant?" she said. "If you look things up, you remember them."

"You must have really wanted to remember that, to have it tattooed over your ass."

"The small of my back, if you don't mind?" she said. "Go take your shower or you're going to smell like sex."

"Is that a real axiom? Or did you just make it up?" he said.

"No, I didn't make it up."

"Well, why do you know stuff like that?"

"We used to spend these long dull Sundays at my grandparents when I was young. I'd get bored sometimes and since my sisters were older than me, I'd be by myself for hours. My Grandmother was scholarly and had this huge *gringo* dictionary. I'd spend all day going through it."

"No wonder you're such a good student. You actually studied for fun." he said. "So, you found this Latin saying in a *gringo* dictionary?"

"My Nana taught me that power resides in certain languages." she said. "Latin, Hebrew, Sanskrit, some others. I wanted to remember it in the Latin. So I wrote it down on my arm with a ballpoint pen to remember it."

"How did it end up tattooed over your,... the small of your back? It's unusual for a woman to get a tattoo. Especially there." he said.

"That was my father's influence. He said that maybe I should get it tattooed somewhere, so I'd always remember it. He didn't think that I'd really do it, at least, that's what he told my Mom. They fought about it for days."

"You're not going to tell me what it means, are

you?" he said.

She let out an evil smirk, "No, I said you need to look it up."

"When?"

"Isn't the college library a couple of blocks from here? You can go while I take my shower, now go take a shower."

$$\therefore \; \Omega \; \therefore$$

That fine March evening, MOFA delegates from all over the southwest gathered at the conference hall on the campus of Rocky Mountain College. They came together with audacious purpose, to ratify and unveil their declaration of independence and to launch their *chicano revolucion.*

Rosalie Sandoval had waited long enough for Emiliano to return to the motel room. She was the MOFA chapter president for God's sake and had to be present at the ceremony. She walked past the meager campus security at the entrance to the conference hall. As she waited in the short line, she noted with suspicion the pair of armed *gringo* security guards and wondered how likely it was that someone might end up getting shot. Just then, someone tapped her on the shoulder.

"Sorry I'm late." said Emiliano.

"What took you so long?"

He held out his forearm with the Latin saying written in ballpoint pen.

"I had to get someone to help me find it. "Webster's Twentieth Century." he said.

"So you know what it means now?"

"Yeah. And I won't forget it either."

Rosalie leaned over and kissed him, "That's my man."

"Oh, and I saw something cool in the window of a thrift store on the way back and it gave me an idea."

Before he could finish, Emiliano recognized the approach of Jesus Duran, one of the local *Mofasistos* who provided security for the meetings of *la camara*.

"Hey man, Where you been?" said Duran.

"I've been sick as a dog, man." said Emiliano.

"Well, you're here now. That's what counts."

"Any others from the bar-b-que get sick?"

"No one that I've heard of."

"No one?" said Emiliano.

"I hope not, my aunt catered it." said Duran. "You two had better get in there."

As Rosalie and Emiliano walked inside the conference hall, Luiz Vargas's penetrating voice was slathered over the public address system.

"Tonight, we make history. As representatives of *la raza*, we unveil *El Plan Espiritual de Aztlán*, the founding document for a new nation. Comprised of the territory stolen by the *gringo* conquests. Tonight, we establish a revolutionary homeland for *la raza,* a homeland based upon justice for *la gente* and the freedom of our indigenous spirituality."

There was cheering mixed with polite applause.

"Now I'll read *El Plan Espiritual de Aztlan* before it is put to you for ratification." said Vargas.

.·. Ω .·.

"Those institutions which are fattened by the sweat of our brothers to provide employment and political pork barrels for the *gringo* will do so only as acts of liberation and for *La Causa*. For the very young there will no longer be acts of juvenile delinquency, but revolutionary acts." Vargas said with an uplifted inflection to cue applause.

The audience complied.

"Now, the article on Actions to be taken." said Luiz Vargas. "Number one, Awareness and distribution of *El Plan Espiritual de Aztlan*. Presented at every meeting, demonstration, confrontation, courthouse, institution, administration, church, school, tree, building, car, and every place of human existence."

Emiliano leaned over to Rosalie.

"This next section is my cue." he said.

"How are you going to do this? she said. "It'll get back to Aguirre and you'll loose your student deferment."

"If we can't prevent this student boycott, my deferment is gone anyway."

"Everyone will know it's you."

"Like I told you, I stopped at that thrift store on the way back. You never know what you'll find in those places. I'll be back."

Emiliano headed for the rear of the hall.

"Number two, September sixteenth, the anniversary of Mexican Independence, a national walk-out by all *Chicanos* of all colleges and schools to be sustained until the complete revision of the educational system."

Aztlánicon:
A Dangerous Precipice Of Vanity

The response of the crowd was ambiguous, but Vargas pressed on.

"Number three, self-defense against the occupying forces."

"Excuse me." a voice interrupted. Everyone turned around to the microphone in the rear of the hall. Standing at the microphone was a bizarre figure wearing a Mexican wrestler's mask. There was scattered, nervous laughter.

"Yes, *Mazorra* the wrestler, if you have a question, please wait until I've read the entire document." said Vargas.

"Excuse me, but I've got a problem with that 'sustained until the complete revision of the educational system." said the masked man.

"First, who are you and where are you from?"

"As you said. I'm *Mazorra*."

There was more laughter.

"From?"

"*Aztlán.*"

"Alright, let's get this over with. You were saying?" said Vargas.

"I say we strike out the part about sustaining this boycott until the educational system is revamped."

"Yes, what about it?" said Vargas.

"If *chicanos* boycott college until the educational system is revamped, then we're not going to be going to college anytime soon."

"Liberating Aztlán will involve struggles and sacrifices."

"Spoken like someone who won't be doing any of the sacrificing." said the masked man.

Antonin Zopenco suddenly knew who this character was.

"The liberation of Aztlán is not going to result from this *pinche* boycott." said the maked man. "You're going to put many innocent people at risk with no beneficial outcome."

"What do you suggest we do instead?" said someone in the crowd.

"Nothing." said the masked man.

There was a lot of grumbling with much voiced disagreement, Mazorro let it settle down.

"At least we let the *gringos* think we are doing nothing." he said.

Luiz Vargas interrupted, "*El Plan Espiritual de Aztlán* has already been written. Much time and hard work has gone into it's drafting. This should have been brought up during *la camara.*"

"It was addressed during *la camara.*" said Mazorro.

Now, Luiz Vargas knew who this character was.

The masked man took the microphone off the stand and addressed the crowd.

"*La gente*,... This student boycott will not bring *Aztlán* any closer to us. It will bring swift defeat and misery to *la raza.*"

"Excuse me,... Come to order." said Vargas.

"Brothers and sisters, please hear me out before this whole thing goes too far and can't be undone. Please." said the masked man.

Aztlánicon:
A Dangerous Precipice Of Vanity

"Security. Send for security." Vargas said.

"Sometimes, things need to be said that no one wants to hear. That's why I have to wear this fucking mask. If you know who I am, I can't say what needs to be said"

"Security." Vargas said even louder.

"What is it that needs to be said?" said someone from the crowd.

The masked man looked at his forearm and read from it, "The drops hollow the rock by frequent falling, not by force."

"What the hell is that supposed to mean?" Vargas said.

"We will only be able to take on the *gringos* by staying below their radar, not this boycott foolishness."

"Foolishness? You're saying our *revolucion* is foolish?" said Vargas.

"No, I'm saying this *chicano* student boycott is foolishness."

Two *gringo* security guards arrived from opposite directions, both with handguns drawn; unsure of what was going on They cautiously inched toward the masked man, a standard response to this kind of situation.

"Put your hands up." said one of the guards.

The masked man complied.

"What's going on here?" said the other guard.

"He's trying to take us all hostage." yelled Antonin Zopenco, concealed behind a group of delegates.

The masked man turned and pointed toward Zopenco.

Aztlánicon:
CODEX IV

"He lies! I'll show you what this is about." said the masked man as he reached into his pocket and started to pull something out.

Zopenco shouted, "He's got a gun!"

Both security guards shot and the masked man fell to the floor. There were screams and panic ensued. People rushed for the exits. Rosalie fought her way over to where the masked man was on the floor. By the time she got there, the *gringo* security guards had already pulled the mask off of Emiliano.

"Look, it wasn't a gun at all." said one *gringo* guard. "It's one of those little brown Virgin statues."

"He got shot over a statue? Stupid Mexican." said the other *gringo* guard.

"Careful, I think they want to be called Chicanos."

For This Shall Continue With Thee

1969
Waltonville, California

2 A BASTARD SHALL NOT ENTER INTO THE CONGREGATION OF THE LORD: EVEN TO HIS TENTH GENERATION SHALL HE NOT ENTER INTO THE CONGREGATION OF THE LORD.
~ DEUTERONOMY 23

With the hot water gently pelting her body, Rosalie Sandoval marveled that the shower did indeed make her feel better, that was until the hot water ran out. She flung aside the mineral stained shower curtain and stepped out of the tub. She staggered and caught herself on the sturdy towel rack. After her balance reestablished, she turned off the water and stood in front of the mirror with the cool air against her positively electric skin. Her hands tenderly cupped her breasts which had become fuller and more sensitive, much more sensitive. She slowly traced her fingers over her enthused nipples, which had turned a darker brown. Rosalie had little doubt at what the signs implied.

∴ Ω ∴

Poco despues, Rosalie sat under the *encina* oaks on campus, Emiliano laid with his head in her lap. Rosalie gently played with his hair as she told him of her suspicions.

"You're pregnant?" said Emiliano as he bolted up. "We only did it that once in Denver."

"Twice!" she said, angered that he'd forget.

"Oh, that time in the hospital. I was sedated." he explained. "So, we only did it twice."

"Twice is apparently enough."

Still not used to his stiff right leg, Emiliano repositioned himself using the cane that was now his constant companion. It was an enduring reminder that Colorado didn't require campus security guards to qualify as marksmen, if it did, Emiliano might be dead. At least now, he was no longer threatened by the draft.

"What should we do?" said Emiliano.

"I don't know which will hurt my mother more, having a child out of wedlock or aborting the fetus." said Rosalie.

"How come when you're going to give birth, it's a child, and when you're going to have an abortion, it's a fetus?" he said.

"I guess abortion is easier to consider when you think of it as something other than a child." said Rosalie. "But if I have an abortion it's got to be secret. It will kill my mother if she finds out."

"Some radical revolutionary you are." said Emiliano. "Do you think it's possible to conduct a revolution without your mother getting upset?"

Rosalie smiled at him, filled with the warmth of his capacity to make her laugh. He was not the educated ideal she'd imagined herself ending up with, but, he was a thoughtful, considerate young man and not at all bad to look at. But most of all, he could make her laugh. That alone would keep her warm through the long wet winters of the central coast, *revolucion* or not.

"Like I said, what should we do? Get married?" said Emiliano.

That said, Rosalie's eyes welled up with tears as she

looked at him with reverence. She had no idea that men like this still existed.

"What's wrong. Why are you crying?" said Emiliano. "You don't want to marry me?"

"I don't know." said Rosalie. "If it means that my life's over and I have to give-up everything that I've worked for, then I'd have to say no, I don't want to get married."

"Fair enough, but why are you crying?"

"Because I'm amazed that you'd even stay here and talk about this with me. A lot of *chicanos* would be gone already, before I'd pronounced the 't' in pregnant."

"That will change when this is truly *Aztlán*. Once the homeland takes root the *hermanos* will see that we must stand up and be responsible for the children we father."

Rosalie immediately stopped sobbing.

"That's just about the dumbest thing I've heard you say."

"You just don't know me well enough yet. I'm capable of saying much stupider things."

"You're right, I don't know you well enough and you're the father of my child. I'm at a crossroads here."

"Do you mean deciding whether you're carrying a child or a fetus?" He took her hand and said, "You're not alone in this."

Rosalie Sandoval looked around for hidden cameras, this had to be some kind of cruel joke.

∴ Ω ∴

Although her parents didn't consider Emiliano any sort of catch for their youngest daughter, they admired the fact that the young man stepped forward to acknowledge his obligations as the baby's father, that was a rare quality in the current generation. Both of Rosalie's older sisters had babies out of wedlock, the men that made them pregnant didn't stick around. Rancher Sandoval was especially fond of this young man that stood up to take responsibility.

Emiliano's willingness to marry Rosalie also presented a wonderful opportunity for *Señora* Sandoval. It was perhaps the last chance in her lifetime to have a 'legitimate' grandchild. She imagined her legitimate grandchild on display to the other parishioners. Finally, she could hold her head high, or, at least, higher. But all of this could only happen if Rosalie married this rare young man before she began showing. The timing would be tricky. The wedding couldn't take place here in town, people would keep track of the interval between the wedding and the birth. It would be obvious that Rosalie was pregnant at her wedding. Even though that was a common situation, it would tarnish the luster of the whole legitimate grandchild fantasy.

A secret ceremony was settled upon to be performed by Father Max, the brother of *Señora* Sandoval, who was a junior priest at the parish down in Hollenger. It was to be the smallest wedding ceremony in parish history; with no record of it anywhere, it wasn't even penciled in on the weekly-planner.

Even though the circumstances were awkward, *Señora* Sandoval smiled through every millisecond of the secret ceremony. As far as the rest of the world was concerned, she was going to have a legitimate grandchild.

∴ Ω ∴

In the weeks that followed the secret wedding, Emiliano Salamanca became a celebrated member of the

Sandoval family.

"You must live here with us, at least until you're done with school." said *Señora* Sandoval.

"Mama, we were going to get a place of our own."

"Are you going to quit school?"

"No, but there's day-care available."

"Nonsense. How are you going to afford day-care? You can't even afford rent."

"We'll manage somehow."

"Besides, my grandchild is not going to be handled by some uncaring, indifferent day-care people." said *Señora* Sandoval. "And besides that, we are just getting to know Emiliano and you want to take him away from us."

Rosalie looked at Emiliano, seeking his opinion. Flattered by the attention, he found it difficult to imagine a downside and indictated his agreement.

"Alright, but we don't want to live here in the house." said Rosalie.

"We're going to re-convert the tool house back into living quarters." said *Señora* Sandoval.

"What about the tools?" said the rancher.

"Your father is going to take care of that right away." said *Señora* Sandoval as she glared at her husband.

Ranchers don't survive long in this world by wasting their energy on struggles that cannot be overcome. Rancher Sandoval was no different. He slowly rose from his chair and looked at Emiliano.

"Well, son. It seems like we better go out back and take some measurements."

"Yes, sir, I think we had better get right to that." said Emiliano as he slowly got up with the help of his cane. He leaned over, kissed Rosalie and then limped out behind the rancher. *Señora* Sandoval leaned back in the sofa and imagined herself cradling her new grandchild. In that moment, all was right with the world.

So it came to pass that Emiliano and Rosalie Salamanca settled into the re-converted tool house which was well-made and of generous dimension, much more generous than anything Emiliano had ever lived in. The modifications by the rancher made the place more than livable and he was almost able to dispel the musty old odor. It would have been his crowning achievement, had he not fallen short of the mark. Knowing that his wife would never settle for her grandchild living in anything less than perfect conditions, the rancher knew that his immediate future would be occupied with getting rid of that odor.

The tool house served the newlywed couple well during that mild summer and into the first semester of the new school year. With the draft no longer an issue, Emiliano and Rosalie actually looked forward to the upcoming *Chicano* student boycott.

$$\therefore \Omega \therefore$$

It was a brisk, damp Tuesday morning on the Encarnacion campus, September 16, 1969. A small cluster of *Chicano* students, most wearing brown berets, stood in symbolic solidarity with *Chicano* students all over the secret homeland of *Aztlán*. The day of the Grand Bold Gesture had arrived.

Emiliano stood at the edge of the small crowd with his weight on one leg. He leaned heavily against the shepherd staff his rancher-in-law had won from a *Basque* shepherd in a poker game over in Los Banos. At the time, Sandoval thought he'd gotten the lesser part of the deal.

Aztlanicon
For This Shall Continue With Thee

But the staff suited Emiliano well and comforted him so much that he came to view it as a very valuable asset. The change brought about in Emiliano was almost magickal. The staff, along with the thick beard he'd accumulated gave off the air of a prophet, a perception he exploited at every opportunity.

Rosalie stood proudly with her husband for what seemed like hours with swollen belly and ankles. Beginning her third trimester, she was a living embodiment of the vast, unfathomable capacity of women. Against her better judgement, she stood and listened to what Antonin Zopenco had to say.

Zopenco stood atop a fake adobe bench in the quad and read a statement, secretly prepared for the gathering.

"As mandated in *El Plan de Aztlán*, on this anniversary of Mexican Independence, we institute a national walk-out by all *Chicanos* of all colleges and schools to be sustained until the complete revision of the educational system to meet the needs of our community. So, until the *gringos* meet our demands we *chicanos* are on strike. Let's go!"

As the small, but surly crowd turned to walk off campus, Emiliano and Rosalie were suddenly at the forefront of the walkout.

It took everything that Emiliano was worth to stay at the head of the group; Rosalie walked slowly at his side, she didn't once reach out to aid him. Later, it would be said of the incident that it looked like a gimpy Che Guevarra and a pregnant *Virgen* leading Israel out of Egypt.

It didn't escape Zopenco that if the press were there taking photos, those photos would show Salamanca leading the historic *chicano* walkout. In one of the first internal power struggles of the fledgling *revolucion*, Zopenco rushed to the head of the mob.

"Come on everyone, *viva la huelga*! *Viva Aztlán*.

Let's go!" said Zopenco, as he waved on the crowd.

Emiliano and Rosalie looked at each other and rolled their eyes. They let the crowd pull away.

"If you want to stay with them, I'll catch up with you later." he said.

"Fuck them. If they want to follow that *pindejo*, let them." she said. "I've got to sit down."

He leaned on her as they hobbled over to a bench in the quad.

"Well, it's begun now." said Rosalie.

"I'll bet the *gringos* have stopped everything and they're restructuring the education system as we speak." said Emiliano.

"The schools are going to lose money if the *chicanos* don't attend classes."

"They're doing just what the *gringos* want." he said.

"What do you mean?"

"They want to keep us out of their colleges." said Emiliano. "Keeping us down is the cost of doing business as usual. Why would the *gringos* want educated *chicanos*? Like they'd have a *chicano* Attorney General or anything like that?"

"I guess they wouldn't. So what do we do now?" she said.

"I guess we have to wait and see if the walkout has any impact."

$$\therefore \; \Omega \; \therefore$$

Too far away to hear anything of the historic *chicano* walkout, Rudolpho Aguirre mingled at the 'second

For This Shall Continue With Thee

tuesday' faculty mixer, held in a reception area atop the grassy knoll next to the administration building.

"Where did this walk-out nonsense come from?" said the Dean of Students. "You're their faculty advisor, you couldn't advise them against this?"

"Believe me, I tried." said the untenured Aguirre. "It's the passion of youth. They blindly follow their hearts."

"They don't even realize how fortunate they are to even have *chicano* studies." said the Dean.

"If the *chicanos* are going to boycott, what the hell do we need a *chicano* studies department for? said the head of the alumni association.

"Who else gives a shit, but *chicanos*? We could use that money to help us comply with Title 9." said the Chancellor of Athletics.

As the clique moved away in deep discussion about how to best reapportion the *chicano* studies budget, Rudolpho Aguirre was suddenly aware of his tenuous position. As he stood on the grassy knoll and drank the *cuba libre*, he could see Rosalie and Emiliano sitting together in the quad. What a bizarre sight they made. Not just bizarre, tragic. Rosalie was the brightest student he'd encountered, but she was more to him, she was a bronze Madonna, a living symbol of the Sainted Mother of *Aztlán* and she was bloated with the fucking child of that peasant Salamanca. Reportedly they were man and wife.

∴ Ω ∴

In the distance, Rosalie could see Rudolpho Aguirre watching the crowd of brown berets march off campus. She wondered if he was satisfied that he was able to manipulate things enough to bring about this foolish action. She felt justified in judging him harshly, he was her mentor and she expected more of him.

Aztlanicon

$$\therefore \Omega \therefore$$

An inescapable reality of any secret revolution is that hardly anyone is aware of it, the Great *Chicano* Walkout of 1969 proved no different and went largely unnoticed by the *gringos*. Just as the Salamancas expected, the *huelga* was a disaster. Some of the *Chicano* strikers stubbornly held out as much as three weeks before returning to campus, with their tails between their legs.

Rosalie continued as a full time student until her water broke during her last final of the semester. Fortunately she'd completed enough of the exam to receive a passing grade. Not her best work, but a remarkable accomplishment just the same. The school retired the chair.

Through a difficult labor that spanned the entire night, Rosalie gave birth to a baby the following sunrise, on *Dios de Guadalupe*. It wouldn't have been difficult to imagine a name if it had been a girl, but the child had a penis. They named it Nestor after no one in particular, they simply liked the sound of Nestor Salamanca.

As *Señora* Sandoval stood weeping with the legitimate newborn in her arms, Emiliano gazed upon his son for the first time. It was amazing to him that this new being had emerged from his wife. He looked at Rosalie, who was exhausted and disheveled. He was humbled by her strength and endurance, how she labored through the night while he napped in the next room with a pillow around his ears. No one was perfect.

$$\therefore \Omega \therefore$$

During the summer that followed, Emiliano grew weary of being lame and vowed to accomplish something in life,... anything. The problem was that he had no idea what to do with himself in his current condition. Guidance was needed, so Emiliano went to rancher Sandoval, who was overseeing the laborers in his fields.

The rancher was seated in one of the two director

chairs that were lined with weathered canvas, under a large market umbrella made of weathered canvas. Between the chairs was a thin little folding table with cups and a pitcher.

"Sir, I want to contribute in some way." said Emiliano.

"Sit, *m'hijo*." said the rancher as he poured a cup of *lemonada* and handed it to Emiliano. "Is it alright if I call you *m'hijo*?"

"It is if I can call you *Popa*."

"Deal."

Not a single worker in the Sandoval fields was aware of the significance of that moment between the rancher and his son-in-law. The field workers were concerned with their backs holding out or wondering what might befall them as they returned home that evening.

"You already contribute, *m'hijo*. You make Rosalie happy. You've given my wife a grandchild that counts at her church."

"Those are important things, but, I want more out of life." said Emiliano.

"What more is there really?"

"I don't know exactly." said Emiliano. "I've decided that I'm not going back to that *pinche* school."

"*Viva huelga*, huh?"

Emiliano laughed with this father-in-law.

"Yeah they haven't revamped the educational system yet. *Viva huelga*."

"What about Rosalie?"

"She'll continue, at least for now. She's the scholar in the family."

"She's always been that, and then some." said the rancher.

"They're not going to draft me all messed up like this and I've got some money from the legal settlement to work with."

"What do you plan to do?"

"That's my problem. I don't know. I just know I want to do something with my life. I want to build something that will last beyond my time here. Something my son can point to and say 'my father made that'."

"You don't want much." said the rancher. "These days a father is lucky if his son refers to him at all. I pray that you have a relationship like that with your son."

"I'm going to try." said Emiliano. "Is that the kind you'd have if you had a son?"

"I can only imagine. I've tried to have that kind with my daughters."

"You seem to have a good relationship with Rosalie."

"We're very close. She's my little *princesa*"

"This is off the subject, but, did you really suggest she get that tatoo?"

"Don't even bring that up. My wife was so angry she cooked with the hottest peppers at every meal she could. I couldn't eat at home for a week."

Though the relationship was merely by law and not by blood, rancher Sandoval welcomed Emiliano under his wing like the 'son-he-never-had'. Emiliano was happy to be with the 'rancher-he-never-had'.

Aztlanicon
For This Shall Continue With Thee

$$\therefore \; \Omega \; \therefore$$

Because of his wounds, Emiliano couldn't contribute much physically to the working of the ranch, but what he couldn't accomplish with his mangled leg he made up for with his mind. Emiliano grew up in farm labor camps and temporary housing and it gave him a rare perspective on the big picture of farm labor. Much to the rancher's joy, his new son-in-law soon displayed an affinity as *el jeffe segundo*, the second boss, a true seat of power on a working ranch. *El jeffe segundo* was the overseer of the laborers. He rounded them up, provided them with shelter, provided them with discipline.

Although well versed from the migrant worker's side of things, Emiliano now had a glimpse of the labor situation from the rancher's side. He could see why a chasm existed between the ranchers and their laborers.

El segundo decided to exploit his rancher-in-law status and began to canvass the other local ranchers to find out what they needed in the way of migrant labor for their operations to run smoothly.

"Sorry about how cramped this 'gator' is. You look pretty bad off with the stiff leg and all." said rancher Brooks, a crusty, hard-ass old timer who specialized in strawberries.

"That's alright. It's just the way it is. My mom raised me not to mope around because things are not how we'd want them to be. She used to say 'deal with things the way they are'."

"Your mother sounds like a wise woman. I wished I'd known her."

"You could've if you'd wanted. She picked berries here quite often. I played around in these fields until I was old enough to be put to work. "

"And look at you now, *el segundo*. Father of the Sandoval family heir."

"That's all *prima*. All I really wanted was Rosalie."

"How is she?"

"Back at school. Working real hard on her thesis."

"Please give her my regards. How come you're not back at school?"

"Someone's got to observe the walkout."

The *anglo* rancher didn't quite know how to take that.

"Just kidding. I plan on going back when I can get around better."

The *anglo* accepted it at that and moved on.

"So until then, you're going to be *el segundo* and give the Sandovals grandchildren." said Brooks.

"Something like that."

"Not a bad life."

"Sir, if I might ask, how is the field laborer situation for you?"

"Sporadic, at best. It's always been that way.

"Do you think that you and the other growers in the area could stand to see it be more stable?"

"Sure, but how is that going to happen?"

"I have some ideas on the subject."

"Any ideas you may have are going to have to get passed Poncho Calderon. He's the lynchpin. If he's onboard, the rest of the *coyotes* will be ripe for whatever. At least the *coyotes* I deal with."

Aztlanicon
For This Shall Continue With Thee

∴ Ω ∴

The only light visible on that moonless night was coming from the headlights of Sandoval's old Ford pickup. The truck was pointed east and the headlights illuminated the long undulating rows of artichokes overwhelmed by a slow, damp fog. The artichoke fields were to the south of Waltonville, across the river, which was more like a creek that time of year. The artichoke is a robust crop which, unlike strawberries, are given a wide birth. Between the rows was enough space to easily drive a pickup, which is what made the artichoke fields such a good choice for what Emiliano had in mind, it was much more convenient than driving all the way up into the mountains.

"Who thought we'd live to see Pancho Calderon on his knees in the *alcachofa* fields." said Emiliano as the thin veil of fog wafted by.

"Fuck you Salamanca. You pussy gimp." said the large middle aged man who was on his knees, bound with his hands behind him, covered with a crust of the damp chicken manure that filled the pickup bed.

"You should have just gone along with the revolution, Pancho."

Pancho didn't even know that he was severely allergic to something in chicken manure. His eyes began to swell up until he verged on looking asian.

"Is it too late to go along with it now?" said Pancho.

"Yes, Pancho. It's too late now. You made us bring your ass all the way down here and look, you're covered in chicken shit."

"I didn't think you'd actually go through with it."

"Guess what, Pancho, I'm going through with it."

"This isn't the *coyote* way, Salamanca." said

Calderon as he veinly tried to remove the chicken manure that covered his swollen face."

"Soon, your kind of *coyote* will be all gone. My kind will be all that's left. Hell yes,... this is absolutely the *coyote* way." Emiliano nodded to his henchman and then turned toward the truck.

The shot rang out through the fog that blanketed the moonscape field. Emiliano heard two distinct echos as he hobbled back to the pickup. The henchman hurried to open the door for *el jefe,* then got behind the wheel and drove slowly into the fog, the shepherd staff sticking out the passenger side window.

"*Jefe*, if I might ask something." said the henchman. "Why did we just kill Señor Calderon?"

"It was rumored that he was working with the *gringos*." lied Emiliano.

"So we kill people over rumors?" said the henchman. "I mean, was it true?"

"We'll never know, but you've heard the old cliche, where there's smoke, there's fire."

"Yeah, but what if he wasn't working with the *gringos* and he died for nothing."

"We all die for nothing." said Emiliano. "Relax, *carnal*. Poncho Calderon is only the first of many casualties of the *revolucion*. If it was a mistake,... well, you have to expect that mistakes are bound to happen. It's revolution, man."

∴ Ω ∴

Because their world was awash with harsh competition and viscious infighting, Emiliano found that the *coyotes* of the region were ripe for enlistment in the righteous *revolucion*. Once he explained the *Aztlán* dream, the *coyotes* welcomed the lofty vision for hollowing out the stone of *gringo* oppression. Rosalie recognized that this movement her husband had started should have a name to rally around. They settled upon *la tuberias*, the waterpipe.

Once the vortex began, the *coyotes* gathered around *la tuberias* like cotton candy gathers around a paper cone. It rapidly blossomed into a fertile breeding ground of underground alliance. But, despite the heart warming qualities of fulfilling the noble cause, the *coyotes* welcomed the money even more. Expansive commerce mixed with the flavor of *revolucion* proved to be a seductive tide that aroused all.

Emiliano Salamanca became the man to deal with in central *Califas*. Even though the rank and file of *la tuberias* swelled to the point of being an entity in it's own right, there were some in the *coyote* realm that did not buy into the *Aztlán* dream. Through the ruthless zeal of a field general, Emiliano Salamanca justified their elimination with the tidy rhetoric that always proved useful in prosecuting revolution.

Aztlanicon
CODEX IV

∴·ϡ⤙⤚) Ω (⤛⤜ϟ·∴

Things Such As These Said The Sinners In Hell

ϡ⤙⤚⤛⤜ϟ

1971
Waltonville, California

16 BUT THE CHILDREN OF ADULTERERS SHALL NOT COME TO PERFECTION, AND THE SEED OF THE UNLAWFUL BED SHALL BE ROOTED OUT.

~ BOOK OF WISDOM: 3

Following her last class of the day, Rosalie went to pick up Nestor at the mobile classroom that had been converted to a childcare center. She was braced to atone for any trouble he might have gotten into that day, as was often the case when she left him there. Rosalie was stunned when she walked in and saw that Nestor was nowhere to be seen.

"Where's my son?" she said to Mrs. Fountaine, the childcare supervisor.

"Professor Aguirre said that you were busy with something and that he was supposed to bring Nestor to you."

"And you let him take my son?"

"Well, he is a member of the faculty."

"How dare you hand over my child to anyone but me or his father."

"Don't yell at me. You're lucky we even look after your little wetback brat. In fact, don't bring him back here. He's not welcome."

166

Aztlanicon
Things Such As These Said The Sinners In Hell

Rosalie considered how badly her life would change if she dropped this woman where she stood. She couldn't get bogged down in this drama, she had to find her son. At that desparate moment, the best Rosalie could do was a potent 'stink eye'.

$$\therefore \Omega \therefore$$

Rosalie barged into Rudolpho Aguirre's office without bothering to knock. It took a few moments, but, when Antonin Zopenco finally realized what was going on, he grabbed the child with his left hand and backed into the dark corner of the room, brandishing a straight razor in his right hand.

Rosalie calmly turned toward Aguirre.

"Why is this *maricón* holding a razor up to my baby?"

"Perhaps he is going to shave him." said Aguirre. "Is that what you're going to do, Zopenco? Shave him?"

"No, I'm going to slit his fucking little throat, Professor."

Rosalie calmly turned toward Aguirre and said, "What do you want?"

"How do you know we don't want to slit his fucking little throat?"

"Because you'd have done it already. What do you want?"

"I hardly see you any more."

"I'm married, I'm a mother, I'm a full time student."

"You're also the revolution's greatest hope. You should be giving birth to our future leaders. Not common little peasants like this one."

"What do you want Aguirre?"

"I want you to carry my child."

"I already have a child."

"We can change that in a matter of moments. Show her Zopenco."

Zopenco held the razor to the child's throat.

"You're not going to kill my baby. Not here in your own office."

Aguirre walked over to Zopenco and took the child from him.

"You're right. I'm not going to kill the child, yet."

"I didn't think so."

"But, surely there must be something that would convince you. Zopenco, anything to suggest?"

"Why not cut off his little thumbs?" said Zopenco.

"That is an inspired idea." said Aguirre as he leaned the child over an end table and held Nestor's little hand down on it. He motioned for Zopenco to come to him. As Zopenco walked, Rosalie could suddenly envision them actually doing this. If she could envision it, it could really happen. It was time to act.

"Alright, let's get this over with."

"Do you mean to take off his thumbs?" said Aguirre.

Rosalie looked at him like the idiot she thought he was as she layed back on the sofa. She reached down under her skirt to matter of factly remove her panties.

"No, let me do that." said Aguirre as he started to

hand the child back to Zopenco.

"No, give him to me right now." she said as she unbuttoned her shirt. "It's time to feed him. My breasts feel heavy."

Aguirre gazed at her dumbfounded. Rosalie held out her arms to receive the child. "Give him to me." she said.

Aguirre handed the child to Rosalie. Once Nestor was situated on her left breast she got as comfortable as possible as she scooted toward the edge of the sofa to facilitate Aguirre's penetration. She spread her legs for him and then defiantly focussed on her nursing child.

"Alright. I'm ready. Let's get this over with." she said.

"No resistance? No fight at all?" said Aguirre. "I expected more."

"Sorry to disappoint you. Does that mean you're not going to be able to get it up?"

As he looked down upon her laying on his sofa, Aguirre took in the vision of this female student that had so facinated him for the past months. He smiled and said, "I'm not disappointed. I only wish we'd had sex sooner."

"This isn't sex, asshole. This is blackmail."

"Blackmail is such a nasty word. I like to think of it as trying to restore the natural social order."

"Why now, while I'm still nursing my child?" said Rosalie.

"No leverage lasts forever." he said as he caressed the inside of her thighs. "Who knows how long *chicano* studies will last."

"Impregnating me serves the revolution how?"

"Who is a brighter hope for the future of *Aztlán* than you, Rosalie." said Aguirre. "You are among the brightest. Capable of leading them all, if you weren't a woman. And with all of this to offer our glorious *Aztlán*, you breed with this peasant Salamanca."

"You elitist fucker."

"Of course I'm elitist, *querida*. That's how it works. Who else but the elite can bring about revolution?

"You'll leave Emiliano and me alone after this?"

"I swear it."

Rosalie knew he was lying. She moved the child to her right breast and when the flow began she again settled back.

"Alright Professor, why don't you get on with depositing one of tomorrow's leaders in me. I've got to get home and make dinner for my peasant husband."

Rosalie focussed upon her child as Aguirre entered her. She didn't feel him much. She kept her attention on her child, hoping that it wouldn't be much longer. She knew it was over when Aguirre stiffened

"Oh, *querida*." he groaned.

Aguirre stayed in her to maximize the chances for his deposit. After a few moments he withdrew and sat down in his chair. Rosalie bolted up and managed to fasten a couple of critical buttons on her shirt, enough to keep it closed, she pushed down the skirt and grabbed the panties.

"If we're done here." she said.

"Wait don't I get a turn?" said Zopenco, who still held the razor.

"Let her and the child go." said Aguirre, still

winded.

"Now wait a minute. I want in on this." said Zopenco as he walked toward the professor and tried to hand him the razor. "You hold this and let me have my turn."

It was obvious that Aguirre didn't want to handle the razor, but he took it anyway, to disarm the young fool.

"You idiot, Zopenco. This isn't about having your turn with her."

"Then what the hell is it about?

"It's about depositing his seed in me for the good of the revolution." said Rosalie "His seed, not yours."

"If she causes problems over this I'm already involved. I should, at least, share in the prize."

"Don't make me dust off my razor moves." said Aguirre. "It's been a few years, but I can still slice you up without breaking a sweat."

With her child beside her, Rosalie opened the office door and let Nestor hobble outside. Once he was outside, Rosalie turned and looked at Aguirre.

"I hope that you're proud of what you've done."

"Sometimes the ends do justify the means, *querida*."

"This is not over." she said as she closed the door behind her.

Outside the office door, Rosalie picked up the child and began to run across the commons to the horticulture pavilion. She placed Nestor on the ground and ran behind the planting benches. She took a garden hose and squatted low. She placed the spray-nozzle deep in her *vagina* and slowly squeezed the muddy nozzle. Rosalie sobbed deeply as the freezing water flushed her and she examined beneath her for dislodged sperm. Rosalie told herself repeatedly that she'd get even with Rudolpho Aguirre.

$$\therefore \Omega \therefore$$

Later that night at Sandoval's *rancho*, Rosalie got herself and the child settled down from the earlier trauma. After she finally got Nestor to go to sleep, Rosalie went into the bathroom and locked the door, where she remained for at least an hour.

Emiliano knew something was different with her, but thought it was best to let her bring it up herself.

When the bathroom door swung open it became obvious what Rosalie had been doing in there. She looked beautiful, but not herself. She was made up, but not dressed up. Emiliano slowly stood as she stepped out into the room. He looked at her in disbelief.

"Are you going somewhere?"

"Over to the bed."

"And then what?"

"We're going to have wanton sex."

"Are you going to wait for me to look up 'wanton'?"

"I'll make an exception."

"I don't have any rubbers."

"I'll make another exception."

"What's going on Rosalie? You don't want me to wear a rubber? Since when?"

Things Such As These Said The Sinners In Hell

Rosalie could hold back no longer.

"He came in me. I tried to flush him out, but I don't know if it worked."

"What are you talking about?"

"They threatened to cut off the baby's thumbs."

"Who did?"

"Aguirre and Zopenco."

Emiliano grabbed his staff and began to move toward the door. Rosalie embraced him, almost knocking him over.

"Don't leave me alone." she said.

"Don't worry. You'll be safe."

"No. Don't leave me alone. I need you with me tonight."

Even though every component of his being wanted to leave and seek vengeance on his enemies, Emiliano dropped his staff and returned the embrace of his woman. She was his touchstone with the new reality, she'd brought a meaning to his life he'd never known before. He would give up everything for her and it was at that precise moment that she needed him.

Rosalie and Emiliano made love several times that night, until Emiliano was spent and otherwise worthless. If a child resulted from all of that day's coupling, there would be strong reason to believe that the child might be a Salamanca. At least, that was what they agreed upon.

∴ ☊ ∴

Two nights later, even though the moon was out, all that was seen from the highway was the cluster of headlights off in the distance. That's why the fields were such a cozy venue for executions. The isolation given by the long fields of *alcachofas* was impeccable. It could have been field workers performing some service or a horde of *borachos* getting drunk for the weekend. Who was to know that it was revolution business?

The *tuberistos* pulled the two squirming bodies from the moist chicken manure in the back of the pickup truck. Rudolpho Aguirre had a crust of manure that came apart when he hit the ground. He writhed in pain with his hands bound behind him, his left wrist broken from the landing. Antonin Zopenco was face down when he was pulled out of the truck. His nose broke his fall.

Emiliano hobbled to the *tuberistos* clustered around the pitiful wretches on the ground.

"I'm going to give one of you a choice." said Emiliano.

"What kind of idiot peasant are you Salamanca?" said Aguirre, as he spat out the manure that had gotten into his mouth. "You can't do this to me. You know who I am?"

"No, professor. Your choice has already been made." said Emiliano as he pointed the gun at Aguirre's head.

"No, I want to do it." said Rosalie.

Several of the *tuberistos* made way for Rosalie, who'd been standing outside the cluster. She walked toward her mentor and saw him covered in chicken shit. She stood back to avoid getting any on her.

"Well, look at you now." she said.

Emiliano offered her the handgun, which she gladly accepted. "Let's do this." She turned and held it to the side of Aguirre's head. Several of the *tuberistos* standing on the other side quickly moved.

"You can't do this to me. What will happen to the

revolution without me?" said Aguirre.

The gun went off and the great Rudolpho Aguirre shut up for good. Emiliano stood over the lifeless body, the eyes still open, starring off into space. Rosalie handed the gun to her husband and stepped back several steps. Emiliano turned to Zopenco, still on his knees, weeping, the blood from his nose mingled with the chicken shit covering his face.

"It looks like you're the one who gets the choice, Zopenco."

"What choice?"

"You can end up like the professor here or you can give up your thumbs. You've got thirty seconds to decide."

It took Zopenco a few moments to take it all in.

"What kind of choice is that?" he said. "What can I possibly do without my thumbs?"

Rosalie leaned in and yelled, "What did you expect my son to do without his?"

"We were never going to do anything to him."

"Maybe not, but you did enough."said Emiliano.

"Fifteen seconds." said one of the *tuberistas*.

"Please. Don't do this. I was just doing what the professor asked me."

Emiliano held the handgun to Zopenco's forehead.

"Time's up. What's it going to be?"

Zopenco winced in anticipation.

"If you don't choose, I will." said Emiliano as he

cocked the hammer.

"Alright. Take my thumbs."

"Good choice. They're doing amazing things with prosthetics. That's the right word isn't it, Rosalie?"

"That's exactly the right word."

"Things are about to change, Zopenco. Good luck to you."

Rosalie joined Emiliano and they began to hobble toward the pickup, arm in arm, Emiliano glanced at his *el segundo,* Juan Ortiz, and said, "Save the thumbs. We'll hang them in our son's room."

Juan turned with a *machete* in his hand and walked over to Zopenco.

Emiliano and Rosalie moved as quickly as they could toward the old pickup. Zopenco's screaming was so much more than they allowed for. When they got settled inside the truck, with the windows rolled up. Emiliano instructed the driver to take them home.

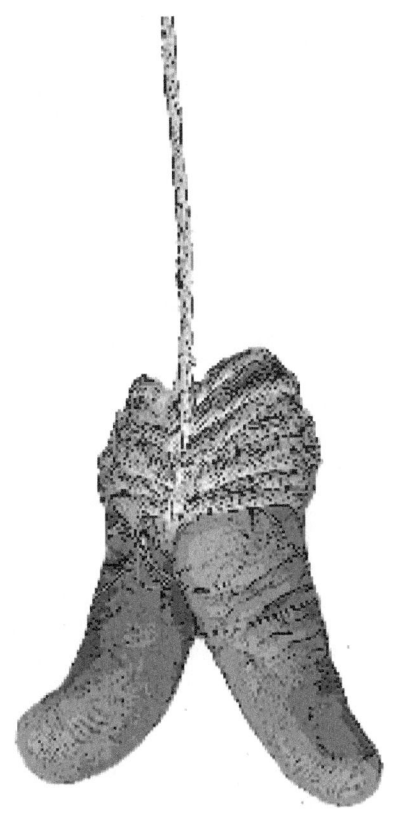

Zopenco's Thumbs
as they hang in Nestor's room.

The Number Of Fools Shall Be Infinite

1971
Branciforte, Aztlán

THE TRUE TEST OF CIVILZATION IS, NOT THE CENSUS, NOR
THE SIZE OF CITIES, NOT THE CROPS- NO BUT THE KIND OF MAN
THE COUNTRY TURNS OUT.
- EMERSON

Judge Falkner Clifford slammed the door to his chambers in the annexed portion of County Branciforte Jail. As he tore off his judicial robe, he glared at the young upstart lawyer, a newbie from the Public Defenders Office. Without bothering to speak, the Judge pointed at the chair, indicating her to sit.

"Ms. Talbert, is it?"

"Yes, sir,... your honor."

"Speak Spanish, do you?"

"Yes,... your honor."

"Well, I'm going to find out how in the hell you got into my court in the first place. But, if you ever want to set foot in this court as anything other than a defendant, you had better forget that you've even heard of Spanish. Do I make myself clear?"

"But, your Honor, my client is looking at serious jail time. You want me to forget that I speak Spanish?"

"Good, you understand."

"I merely pointed out that the interpreter didn't translate something correctly."

"AAAHHHH", yelled the Judge while covering his ears.

The public defender stiffened as she realized that she was out of her league.

"Let's get this straight. You prance into my courtroom and challenge the competence of my translator on the God-damned record in open court. The same translator I've used for the last fourteen years?"

The public defender stared down silently at the floor. She was off to a bad start.

"Do I strike you as someone that would employ an incompetent for fourteen years, Ms. Talbot?"

"No, sir."

"I suggest you think long and hard about this. You're going to risk your career over these people?"

"No, sir."

"*Ándale-pues.*" said the Judge.

The fresh lawyer was intelligent enough to realize that she was being tested. She considered her student loans, her fledgling law practice and the newly acquired coastal home three blocks from the Lighthouse.

"Excuse me, sir, but, I don't understand Spanish."

The Judge smiled. "I see potential in you, Ms. Talbot. Your quick on the uptake -- manageable."

She nodded sheepishly.

'We're going to reconvene and no matter what you hear in that courtroom, I'm not going to hear another syllable concerning the translation of English into Spanish or vice versa. Not a peep. Is that clear?

Ms. Talbot nodded.

"I didn't hear your answer, Ms. Talbot."

"Yes, your honor. I understand that in your courtroom I don't understand Spanish."

"If you last around here you'll come to see that an expedited system is best for all concerned."

"But your honor, some of these people are facing prison."

They're not going to do hard time. The ones that have skill sets will be put to work. Two and half square meals a day. A place to sleep. Conjugal visits. That's more than what's guaranteed to anyone on the outside."

The young lawyer looked down, as though her world view had been suddenly shattered.

What's wrong, Ms. Talbot? You seem upset."

"Law school didn't prepare me for stocking factory prisons."

"There's alot that law school didn't prepare you for."

The atmosphere was constricted and the new public defender was visibly upset. The Judge didn't care if this was too much all at once. She would either learn or be moved out of the way.

"This globalization garbage is being rammed down our throats." he said. "We have no choice."

Aztlánicon
The Number Of Fools Shall Be Infinite

Judge Clifford waited for a sign of her acquiescence.

"Do we understand each other Ms. Talbot?"

He knew that she had probably come too far, risked too much to abandon her career path and start all over.

"Yes, your honor, I think we understand each other?"

"You think we understand each other?"

"No, we understand each other."

" Good. Now get out of here."

The young public defender left.

After an interval of revival, the Judge readied himself to reconvene the late morning session, donning his judicial robe, envisioning himself clothed with the sovereign power of the state. The Judge took a deep breath, tried to look determined and flung open the gates to hell.

$$\therefore \Omega \therefore$$

"All rise for the Honorable Judge Faulkner Clifford."

Rosalie Salamanca stood up like everyone around her and watched the *gringo* judge enter the courtroom as reluctantly as a janitor would begin the nightshift. He didn't seem to want to be there anymore than she did.

"Alright, call the next case." said the judge.

Rosalie watched as her shackled husband hobbled into the small courtroom in a county orange jumpsuit. Visibly glad to see her, Emiliano smiled. When instructed to stand before the bench he limped heavily on a feeble, court approved crutch.

"Your honor, our office received a complaint charging

Emiliano Salamanca in the execution style murder of
Rudolpho Aguirre, and two felony counts of criminal
neglegence in connection with the loss of the thumbs of one,
Antonin Zopenco."

"Zopenco? Like the lawyer?"

"His son."

The judge looked at Emiliano with pity over his probable
future.

"Do you understand the charges against you?" said the
judge.

The translator turned to Emiliano and asked him in
Español if he understood why he was there.

"That's not what he asked me." said Emiliano as he
turned toward the judge. "I'll save the court's time and
admit that I did these things. There's no need for a trial."

The judge's sigh filled the small courtroom, everyone
could feel the energy of his disappointment.

"This seems like one of the rare interesting ones. You
don't want to deny the charges, in hope that the district
attorney can't make the case against you? It's happened
before."

"I did these things with good reason and in my world
the actions were entirely justified. But now I stand before
you a political prisoner held captive by the *gringo* empire."

"Oh, it's like that." said the judge. "So, you did all of
this by yourself? I mean, a man in your physical condition
might find it difficult to kill one man while taking off the
thumbs of another."

"It's pointless for me to seek justice here, where there is
no justice to be found."

∴ Ω ∴

A thick panel of clear plexiglass between them, Rosalie sat across from Emiliano in the visitor room of the jail, each held a telephone.

"Why don't you deny it like the judge said?"

"No, I don't want there to be any trial."

"What am I supposed to do with you in here?"

"You're going to have to take over and run the *familia*."

She thought about what that meant.

"You're going to promise me that if there is a baby and you have any indication that it's not mine,... Promise me that this bastard will never be the head of the *familia Salamanca*. Swear to me."

"Okay, I swear it, but why are you talking like this?"

"There can't be a trial. There can't even be an investigation."

∴ Ω ∴

The next day Rosalie entered the jail to visit with her husband. She filled in her name on the clipboard and waited in the cold, institutional seating for her name to be called.

"Rosalie Salamanca." said the deputy.

"I'm Rosalie Salamanca."

"The prisoner you're here to see was killed last night trying to escape."

"How's that possible? He was on a crutch."

"That's all the information I have."

∴ ⁘ ⟩ Ω ⟨ ⁘ ∴

To Wander A Labyrinth Of Error

2015
Waltonville, Aztlan

Poolside, oblivious to the chafed vigil of her husband, Lupe Obregon lounged in exquisite nakedness. *Don* Nestor Salamanca shifted in the club chair and scanned the central courtyard of the *hacienda* for plots that were surely in progress. There was always some bullshit reason to come ask *el jeffe* something trivial just to sneak a glimpse of the naked *Doña*.

The time of mutual esteem had evaporated between *Don* Nestor and the henchmen that frequented the *Casa de Salamanca*. Ever since he brought his beautiful young wife to live there, everyone with a penis was under suspicion. Being surrounded by unsavory characters was never a problem before; affiliation with them was a cost of doing business in the *coyote* trade that his father and mother built up. *Don* Nestor had known many of these men since he was young, they were the chosen ones, selected by his father and retained by his mother when she took over the *familia* in the aftermath of the assassination. Now, not one of them was to be trusted.

Nestor knew that they imagined being with her. He loathed that they even had the nerve to harbor such fantasy. He resented their peasant capacity to even rest their eyes upon her, even though he fully understood the urge to look at her; after all, it was looking at her that captured him in the first place. She looked like a goddamned film star, back when they had film stars. But, even though he understood why they would want to look at her, that didn't mean he was going to allow them to oogle his prize. He looked at her reclining upon the chaise and studied her bronze skin as it arrogantly infused the Sun's radiance on this indian summer day. The same radiance his laborers were shielding themselves from the mere length of a *futbol* field off in the distance. If not for a slight chromosome difference, Guadalupe could have very easily ended up as one of the *campasenas* working in the fields, stooped over with an aching back picking crops day after day, surrounded by pesticides, instead of being sprawled out by the pool in this luxurious nakedness. It was precisely the capacity to possess such a prize that elevated him, who else but *el jeffe* could possess such a woman?

This was now his *hacienda,* his fountain and his elegant swimming pool, along with the huge mural on the wall behind it, one of several murals commissioned by his beloved mother, meant to look as if Diego Rivera had painted the heroic icons of the secret Aztlán *revolucion.* *Don* Nestor sat back and listened. Not a human sound could be heard in the hushed courtyard, only the steady drops of water that fell from the marble urn held by a *terracotta* angel. The warrior-like drops tumbled from the urn to the field of battle, which was a small granite boulder taken from the Merced River, just outside the Yosemite boundary. Nestor remembered how the minions complained about hauling that rock in the middle of the night, but that was how *Doña* Salamanca wanted it. So, that was how it happened.

Slowly Nestor opened his eyes and looked at the motto painted onto the large mural. He read the words and grappled with the distance he felt toward them.

THE DROP HOLLOWS THE STONE
FROM FREQUENT FALLING,
NOT BY FORCE.

These were sacred words to the *Doña*, they encoded her vision for the secret revolution of *Aztlán.* Nestor preferred the slogan in Latin, the way it was tattooed upon the small of the *Doña's* back.

Nestor watched the *terracotta* angel pour drops of

water and remembered how it was when the *Doña* was still alive. One after another, the individual drops of water left the lip of the urn and crashed against the granite slab. Nestor was struck by how much larger the hole in the granite had become. The slogan had more meaning if you remembered the granite when it was flat and there was no hole. Usually, the hole went unnnoticed, which itself was testament to the genius of the *Doña's* vision for the *Aztlán* revolution.

Nestor then gazed higher at the votive candles that flickered at the feet of a large statue of the *Virgen de Guadalupe*. The *Doña* had ordered the sculptor to fashion the statue in a way that it could never be misunderstood to be the Virgin Mary. If there was to be misapprehension, it should be toward mistaking her for *Tonantzin*, the Aztec goddess.

For Nestor, the reconquest of *Aztlán* was the dream of his parents. The more he tried to make it his own the more distant it felt. The more he tried to get used to thinking of the *familia* as his, the more this place felt like his parent's *hacienda*, their *revolucion*.

$$\therefore \Omega \therefore$$

As a cool afternoon breeze grazed against the windchimes scattered around the lush courtyard, delicate bell tones were echoed with the tiny goosebumps on Guadalupe's opulent backside. She jiggled slightly to shakeoff the chilling effect. Necks craned, heads turned. Heads that had been doing a good job of not looking like they were looking.

"Get back to work. All of you!" said Nestor.

As the faint snickers of the houseworkers dispelled, the courtyard settled, until, "I just got off the phone with Tijereta."said Eberto Aguirre, *Don* Nestor's loathed half-brother.

Nestor jumped to his feet.

"Not here, come inside." he said as he diverted Eberto away from his naked wife and ushered him indoors.

Guadalupe smiled at the amusing futility. Eberto had seen her naked plenty of times.

Inside the *hacienda*, Nestor lead Eberto to the study. Nestor turned and said, "Alright, what is it?"

"I just got off the phone with Tijereta down in *Tamaulipas*. One of our trucks got jacked again. Everyone's dead."

"What the hell is going on?" said Nestor.

"He says that all the *coyote familias* are having a summit at Paco Izquierdo's place. They want a representative of *Familia* Salamanca to attend to discuss ending the exile." said Eberto.

"Ending of the exile?"

"That's what he said."

"Imagine that. Full membership in the *Ayunta* again."

"You'll finally be a real *Don*." said Eberto.

"I'm already a real *Don*."

"Whatever."

"That's it, you're going down there to this meeting and get things straightened out."

"Why me? You're the *Don*."

"You're in charge of the *familia*'s *coyote* interests. So you'll go down there and set things right." .

"I'm not going down there. Get real. Besides you

only put me in charge because the *coyote* operation has been on autopilot since before either of us were born." said Eberto.

"That's no longer the case."

"No shit, it's no longer the case."

"Look someone's got to go down there to represent our interests at this *coyote* summit."

"They're fucking shooting people down there. I'm only a figure head. So why should I put my ass on the line?"

"So here you go, I'm giving you the real power to go negotiate for our interests." said Nestor.

"Well, I agree that someone's got to go, it's just not going to be me."Eberto said and then left the room.

In anger, Nestor picked up a small glass orb that his mother gave him as a child and threw it against the wall, The orb shattered and the fluid with plastic snowflakes ran down to the floor.

"Leave him, he's weak." said Guadalupe, suddenly at the doorway, a robe draped over her. "You never really made him in charge of anything, he knows that. What did you expect? He's going to sprout *huevos* all of a sudden and go down to Mexico and save your *coyote* business? Is that what you thought?"

Nestor stared at Guadalupe for an moment, he didn't care for the mocking tone in the way she said *Don*. But, despite the intented snipe at him, she still took his breath away. She could have had any man she wanted, how did she end up with him? He realized that he couldn't let her know that he felt this way. He would end up more oppressed than he already was.

"Against my better judgement, I did as my mother asked and took him in the *familia*, now look where we are. How did things get so bad?" said Nestor.

"Because you don't take care of business. You're
trying to pawn it off on Eberto. You should be going
down there yourself. You're the *Don*. It's your
familia."

Nestor seethed as he realized that she was right. If
things were going to be straightened out, he was going to
have to do the straightening. He looked at Guadalupe.
What will she do while he's away at this meeting?
Probably laying around on display for Eberto and
everyone else, or worse.

"You and I are going to Nuevo Laredo." said
Nestor.

"No, I'm not."

"Why not, do you have something else going on?"

Without a word, she turned and headed back to the
courtyard. Nestor followed.

"It'll be like a getaway just for the two of us." he
said as he pursued her through the entertainment room.
As she stopped to open the sliding glass door, she
suddenly turned toward him, her hands on her generous
hips.

"Yeah, a romantic getaway in some sleazy, third
world hell-hole while you meet with your *coyotes*. That
sounds perfect, honey. Why wouldn't I want to do
that?" She turned away and marched back out to the
courtyard. Again, he followed.

"You could be of help to me." he said, trying to
keep up with her, "Everybody has an entourage at these
things. You could be my entourage."

Guadalupe stopped and faced him, "First, one
person doesn't make for an entourage, second, are these
macho *forajidos* going to accept you bringing your wife

to this kind of thing? Aren't you expected to bring a mistress or a hooker or something like that? That's what they do in the movies." she said as she removed her robe, again revealing her naked extravagance.

Nestor inhaled sharply, staggered by the unfairness of the confrontation.

"You could travel under your maiden name." said *Don* Nestor, in search of a context that she would agree with, his voice altered with the fear her beauty held over him, his fear of losing her and the damage that would do to the public image he hasn't even had time to develop yet.

"Do you know how pitiful you sound?" said Guadalupe. "Of course, you don't. If you did you wouldn't do it."

"What do you want from me? I'm just trying to be respectful of what you want."

"The freaking *Don* doesn't ask if you want to go. He tells you that you're going." she said.

"The *Don* told you not to sunbathe out here with nothing on, yet you still do."

"I have sunscreen on." she said.

"There's always loopholes with you." he said. "Eberto could see you, hell, everyone can see you."

"Eberto saw me long before you ever did. I made sure you knew that before I agreed to marry you." She layed face down on the chaise lounge.

Nestor hated that she threw that in his face. Why did she have to keep bringing that up. They used to see each other, all of each other, many times.

"I'm going to the firehouse." He turned to leave and then stopped, "And, you are going with me to

Mexico and that's that. There is no way that I'm leaving you here." He turned and left her there.

With her eyes closed, Guadalupe layed on display, "Run away, run away." she said to herself.

With Nestor gone, the boldest of the house workers and gardeners begin to drift back to better vantage points to watch the beautiful, young *señora*. Suddenly, *Don* Nestor came back out into the courtyard and announced to them, "I can have all of you bastards on your way back to wherever you came from this afternoon. If that's what you want, fine. But, if you wish to continue working here,... you'll get the hell out of here and stay out as long as the *señora* is sunbathing."

He listened to the *bichos* scatter and then turned toward her. "Can you put something on? Please? You're the *Don's* wife, you're supposed to be on my side."

He turned and slouched off.

"Why don't you start acting like the *Don*." she said to herself. She knew that her behavior embarrassed him in front of the workers. She did it to make him pay for the trophy-wife status that she had to endure.

A few moments later the quiet of the courtyard was ruffled by the slam of a car door and the squeal of tires as Nestor drove off with an obvious display of wrathful attitude. Guadalupe thought of how dismayed Nestor would be if he knew how little consequence his angered exits really had.

As the sound of the car trailed off in the distance, Eberto Aguirre emerged from the shadows, pulled a chair next to the chaise and sat. With unambiguous familiarity, he reached over and gently traced the flesh along her spine, across the small of her back, down the cleft of her bronze, shapely ass. She gently moaned, but then impatiently pushed his hand away.

"Not now... Let me get some sun, there's time for that later." she said.

Eberto abandoned the endeavor, he knew from long experience that when Guadalupe Obregon didn't want to do something, there's no convincing her otherwise.

"So, are you going with him?" he asked.

"Not now. We'll talk later."

"Answer my question, are you going with him?"

"Maybe."

"And what am I supposed to do while you're gone."

"I'm not concerned about what you do while I'm away with my husband?" she said. "Do what you do normally, nothing. Wait, I know what you can do, you can patch things up with my sister."

"But, what about us?"" he said.

"What about us? I'm married to your brother."

"My half-brother." he said.

They're interrupted by the ring of Eberto's cell phone.

"Hello?......Alright, I'll be there." He clapped the phone shut.

"That was him. He wants me to meet him at the lake. He needs to talk with me." Eberto said as he reached out to lightly traced along her contours. "But, we both know he doesn't trust me here alone with you."

Guadalupe brushed his hand away, "I wonder why he feels like that?"

Aztlánicon
To Wander A Labyrinth Of Error

Eberto was getting no place with her, but, it wasn't
his style to just slip off in defeat like his pathetic half-
brother, so he slapped a red, angry handprint on her bare
behind and laughed as he walked away.

"*Putamadre*... asshole. Now go, he needs you for
something." she realized what a ridiculous thing she just
said. No one needed Eberto Aguirre for anything. As
she savored the sting on her butt, she watched him leave
and admitted to herself that she didn't regret the time she
spent with Eberto Aguirre, especially since no children
resulted, but that was then and it was ackward to have
him around now. Sure, he was fun, but even back then,
Lupe Obregon saw that Eberto Agguire had no aptitude
as a provider, none at all. He couldn't even provide for
himself much less the manner she had her sights set on.
But, when the heir to the *familia Salamanca* presented
himself to her, that was a different matter entirely.

$$\therefore \; \Omega \; \therefore$$

Following the discovery of the *Aztlánicon*, *Doña*
Rosalie Salamanca brought her sons, Nestor and Eberto,
to this sacred place with the hope of introducing them to
the *milagró*. But, more importantly, she wanted to gently
introduce them to the practice of the *magica divina*. But,
despite her nurturing, the boys would have none of it.
They were devoted to the memory of *Don* Emiliano
Salamanca and their emulation of that memory did not
include praying to some holy spirit supposedly contained
in a tree.

Don Emiliano Salamanca had no room in his life for
things of a spiritual nature, it wasn't that he considered it
nonsense, he had profound respect for *magica divina*,
respect that grew from first hand experience. *Don*
Emiliano's realm extented only as far as the molecular
world. He had both an underworld business and a
revolucion to run. His reality was limited to wielding the
ways of tactical malice and political treachery; or dealing
with the necessity of someone's elimination. *Don*
Emiliano left spiritual matters to the capable hands of his

beloved wife.

In her capacity as *consejera magica*, *Doña* Rosalie secretly piloted *familia Salamanca* along the treacherous timeline of *revoluçion* cloaked as underworld enterprise. For guidance, *Doña* Rosalie relied on different forms of folkloric divination, the progressions and transits of the heavens, the meaning ridden symbols of her weathered old tarot, and the wisdom gyrations of a hematite pendulum. *Doña* Rosalie was adept at extracting meaning from the cosmos around her, meaning that was brought to bear upon issues of the moment.

The seperate and distinct strengths Rosalie and Emiliano brought to their marriage intertwined into a *familia* that was formidable in several dimensions, so formidable that the other *familias* in the regional *coyote* trade weren't left with much; this caused problems. Problems that were not easily solved, even with the practice of *magica divina*. These problems ultimately were dealt with violently, leaving *familia Salamanca* in Nestor's questionable hands.

$$\therefore \, \Omega \, \therefore$$

As Nestor waited for Eberto to show up, he wonderd how everything would be so very different if the *Aztlánicon* had simply appeared on the other side of the tree or up on top where it would have never been seen. None of these people would be down here. All of these candles wouldn't be here. The hundreds of photos and prayers wouldn't be hanging in ziplock bags on the fence, the fence that wouldn't have been built. Instead of a Holy Ground, this all would merely be a rural fishing pier. And even though the phenomenon of the *Virgen Guadalupe* remained a stranger to him, *Don* Nestor acknowledged that there remained the fact of a continuous, almost universal appeal that the *Virgen* held over people.

"What's up?" said Eberto Aguirre.

Don Nestor turned around and saw his half-brother.

"Look around at the site here, and tell me if you notice anything different."

Eberto had never really paid that much attention to this place and was not sure what Nestor meant.

"Seems likes the usual bunch of religious nut cases, shining their mirrors on that tree. Just like they've been doing ever since mom used to bring us here."

"No, I mean, do you notice those stakes in the ground, the ones with the orange markers?"

"Yeah."

"Those are survey markers. Why is this place being surveyed? That's what I want to know, that's what I want you to find out while I'm gone."

"Who cares why this place is being surveyed?"

"I care. Therefore *familia Salamanca* cares. What's wrong with you? Look at all the people that gather here. Like you said, they've gathered here since we were young. Today's a small turnout, but look, even during the middle of the week, on a work day, they come to the *Aztlánicon*."

"I don't believe in that *Virgen Guadalupe* bullshit. I mean she's a cool symbol and everything, but I'm not holding my breath waiting for that tree to do something in my life."

"I'm not either, but, it doesn't matter if we believe in her. They believe in her and they believe that somehow she is contained in that tree over there and that's what makes this place special."

"They're just ignorant, superstitious peasants with weak minds."

"Whatever they are, they gather together, *pindejo*. There is money where people gather. And there is power."

"That sounds like your father talking." said Eberto.

"You never knew my father, but I'll take that as a compliment." said Nestor as he pointed toward the *Aztlánicon*. "These people come from all around to connect with their *milagro* and *familia Salamanca* is about to move into the *milagro* business."

"What's the *milagro* business? We're going to muscle in on the little old ladies and take over their mirror racket?"

Nestor occasionally experienced moments when he did not loathe Eberto, it was when he recognized their mother in him, this was one of those moments.

"If that's the best we can do for now." said Nestor. "This is our territory. We have to control it or it won't stay our territory for long. After we settle that, then we'll move in on the old ladies and the mirrors."

"I still don't know what you mean by *milagro* business, I don't think the tree down there is taking on any partners."

"First things first, I need to know who has been surveying this place and why. Eberto we have to find out who has plans for this place and what those plans are. Then we can figure out how to get in their way. So, by the time Guadalupe and I return, I'd like to know something."

"So, she's really going with you?"

With that single question, it was obvious to Nestor why Eberto remained *el Odio*. No matter how much he may take after their mother, his father always surfaced sooner or later. In an instant, Nestor's meager affection toward his half-brother vanished.

"I know what you're thinking, *pindejo*." said

Nestor.

"You have no idea what I am thinking."

"She's my wife. She picked me, not you,... me. Get over it and move on."

"You don't give me credit for anything. I'm just the 'hated one' in your eyes and all you think I'm capable of is fooling around with your wife."

"Oh come on. We both know you want her."

"Nestor,... been there, done that. Before you even knew who she was."

Nestor's anger swelled within, this was the second time in an hour that he had this pointed out to him. "You had better be very careful about what you say on this subject from here on."

"Let's talk about *la familia* then. Now that you've taken over, it amuses me to watch you flounder around with it. You've got no idea what you're doing."

"Look, *pendejo*, like you said, I'm the *Don* of this *familia* now. I just have to snap my fingers and you're just another dead body they find by the side of the road up in Herkermer Pass."

Eberto looked Nestor right in the eyes and stood his ground.

"Yeah? I guess we'll have to wait and see about that. said Eberto as he turned and walked away.

Nestor yelled after him, "Find out that information while I'm gone."

Eberto turned and looked at him in a manner that made Nestor uncomfortable, a look that Nestor hadn't seen in long time.

Aztlánicon
CODEX V

"Enjoy your trip to Mexico." Eberto said, as he chuckled to himself and disappeared up the trail that lead back to the parking lot.

∴ ·ᶜ✐⌒〗Ω〖⌒✐ᶜ· ∴

Only To Bring Forth Thistles And Thorns
✐⌒⌒✐

2015
Nuevo Laredo, Mexico

Outside Nuevo Loredo, a uniformed driver from Hotel Tamaulipas stood curbside at the airport with a sign that had 'Salamanca' scratched on it. The driver held the sign high as passengers began to file out past the tiresome security checkpoints. The driver perked up considerably as Nestor approached with a stunning woman at his side. In that moment, the young driver pled with his version of God that this be Salamanca, just so he could look at this woman a little longer.

"I'm Salamanca." said Nestor as he held out the luggage claim tickets. The young driver took no notice because he was trained on Lupe like a Doberman sizes up a rabbit. Nestor was sure that this guy's grin couldn't get any wider, not without tearing something.

"You're bringing your wife to Nuevo Laredo, sir?" said the driver.

Nestor dangled the claim tickets in his face. "This isn't my wife. If that's any of your business. Show us to the car and then get our bags."

As the driver took the claim checks, Nestor took Lupe's arm and they began to walk toward the limo.

"Can you believe the nerve of this asshole?" said Nestor as they walked.

"What do you mean? I think it's cute." said Lupe.

"The way he looks at you. He's undressing you with his eyes, right in front of your husband."

"You just told him that I'm not your wife." she said, laughing.

"It's not funny."

"Of course it's funny. Come on, you know I love to be looked at. Being looked at gets me in the mood. Besides, isn't that why you married me? For people to look at?"

"No, I married you so I could look at you. I just didn't realize it would be so much trouble."

"I guess it sucks to have a trophy that won't stay put in the trophy case."

Nestor wondered if his father had this much trouble with his mother.

Entrenched in the back of the limousine, the drive to Nuevo Laredo seemed to take forever. The intense effect she had upon the young driver no longer amused Lupe and his staring in the rearview mirror annoyed her.

"Tell him to put the partition up." she said.

"Hey up there. Put up the screen, we want some privacy back here."

"Right away, sir." the driver said.

As the partition scrolled closed. Lupe expected a display of some sort, but the driver failed to display much of anything. She wouldn't have been so affronted if she knew about the closed circuit television on board.

Under the impression that they were no longer being watched, Nestor and Lupe drifted back into their habitual low grade misery. She languished into a bitchy, hyper-picky mood that found fault with everything that appeared in her sense fields. When she was like that, Nestor knew from experience that nothing he could do was going to be good enough for her. Why couldn't she just give him one of those punitive silent treatments she was so capable of. Her silence would be too merciful toward him, she was only satisfied when he was made to suffer. How could he be so entirely whooped by a woman much younger than he?

2008
Waltonville, Aztlán

During the fall, on a miserable night, Nestor failed to understand the enormous jeopardy his mother placed herself in by being exposed in public. He wondered what was worth all of this risk, especially for a stupid dance contest. But, being the dutiful son, he kept his mouth shut and accompanied her with four bodyguards to the nightclub Salsa Mundo.

The bodyguards were vigilant and scanned the crowd for potential threats, Nestor sat at a table with *Doña* Salamanca and wondered what was taking so long. They couldn't get the *Doña* back home to safety until this contest was over and it couldn't be over unless it had already started. The crowd was so loud that he didn't catch the muffled announcement,

"Here they come." said *Doña* Salamanca, as she stood up and applauded as the contestants entered the dance floor. The bodyguards bristled at the *Doña's* increased exposure and their vigilance became even more intense.

Nestor decided to see for himself what the big deal was and stood up. In that moment the entire universe shifted. There she was, the most stunning creature he'd ever seen, strutting onto the dance floor, hand in hand, with Eberto, who by some existential unfairness was her partner. Nestor was spellbound as a samba began to play and she began to gyrate to the complex rhythm of the music. Nestor wondered how this could be any kind of contest because in his mind she was the only one out there on the floor. How could anyone else stand a chance of even being noticed.

"Mama, I don't know whether to thank you or curse you. You've talked about Eberto and his dance partner for weeks. Now I understand why."

"Yes, she's very beautiful, but more than that, this girl is a rare find. Even though she doesn't fully have a command of it, she carries the power. I can see that she belongs with you at the head of *mi familia,* after I'm gone."

"You've placed me in an ackward position. Now that I know she exists, I have to go after her."

"I was hoping you'd have that reaction."

"But what about *el Odio*?" said Nestor.

"Don't call him that. He's still your brother and it will be upon you to watch after him."

"I'll watch after him, but I'll never believe that he's my brother. He doesn't even look like a Salamanca."

"He's my son, alright. But a girl like that belongs with the *Don*. She doesn't belong with him. I vowed to your father that as long as I had anything to do with it, Eberto would never become the *Don*."

"Why not, if he's your son too?"

"That is another conversation, which I promise we will have."

2015
Nuevo Laredo, Mexico

Nestor languished in the thick silence that filled the rear of the limo. What did his beloved mother see in Lupe that he still didn't see? Of course, she was beautiful, but, that wouldn't be enough to cause Rosalie Salamanca to recommend someone for the heir to her *familia*. Nestor knew that his mother must have recognized something admirable in Lupe and he was determined to discover what it was.

"I want to apologize to you. You were right about making you come along on this trip. It was a dumb idea."

"You didn't want me home alone with Eberto. I understand that. You don't have trust in me."

"I don't have trust in him. But I also know that you don't love me and you married me for the money."

"Half the money. Only half."

Nestor smiled. He almost feared her ability to make him smile.

"Look, I don't want to keep you in some trophy case and I want you to enjoy your youth. Hell, I want to enjoy your youth. Just don't make me look like a fool."

Lupe perked up considerably at this concession. She decided to reward him like she would a dog that learned a new behavior. She glanced over and confirmed the closed partition and then scooted beside him and unzipped his trousers.

"What's this? A moment ago you were punishing me. Now you want to do this?"

She immediately zipped his pants back up.

"Fine. If you don't want that. I tried."

"No, no. I didn't mean that. I'm sorry. You just surprised me, that's all. Please, please continue."

Lupe thought about it for a moment and unzipped his pants and gently coaxed his weasel from it's burrow. Her caress of him was more positive reinforcement than lust, but that would do for Nestor at this juncture. The two became so involved that neither of them noticed the limo come to a stop. As Lupe stimulated her husband neither of them noticed the partition slowly come down, nor did they notice the young driver leering at them, until Nestor opened his eyes. He jumped in the seat, which caused Lupe to gag. She bolted up, startled, gasping for air.

"What is it with you and blow jobs?" she said.

"Excuse me." said the driver.

Lupe turned around, startled.

"Look, I know this is kind of unprofessional. But, you are so hot, and I don't know if I'll ever see you again, and since you're not married. I mean what the hell, right? "

"What are you getting at?" said Nestor.

"Is there any chance you guys might be into a threesome? Instead of giving me a tip,... we could just take care of it right here."

Nestor was affronted. "You little *putamadre*." he said.

Lupe was intrigued by this kid's audacity, perhaps it carried over into his sexual performance. Suddenly she was curious. She looked at Nestor to gauge his reaction.

"Well? You said that you wanted to enjoy my youth. So let's enjoy it. Who's going to know?"

Lupe reached out and again took Nestor in hand. He was unsure of how far to let this go, but if this would make her happy. After she again made him sufficient, she pulled off her panties and turned with her back to Nestor, as she lowered down and took him in. Nestor moaned as he was deliciously enveloped by her and began slowly thrusting. For a few moments she focused on her share of their coupling. After they manage to establish a slight awkward rhythm, she looked at the young driver and motioned for him to present himself.

"Come on, let's see what you've got." she said as Nestor's hands reached around and cupped her still clothed breasts.

The driver suddenly seemed bashful, things had taken a turn he hadn't allowed for. He'd only fantasized about experiencing her without consideration of her experiencing him.

"Come on, you said a threesome." she said.

The driver was under the impression that Lupe was a pro and figured that she wouldn't make a scene over his equipment.

"I hope you won't be disappointed." he said quietly as he slipped over the front seat into the passenger compartment.

As Nestor maintained his stroke into her, Lupe reached out and unzipped the driver's pants and pulled out the smallest penis she'd ever seen, it barely protruded beyond the opening of his pants. She assured herself that that couldn't be the final, actual size of it and so she took him into her mouth and worked to make him bigger. After awhile it felt to her like sucking on a worn down candy cane, except it didn't taste like a candy cane. She removed it from her mouth and got off Nestor in one frustrated motion, everything came to a halt.

"What's this bullshit?" she said. "When you suggested having a threesome, I just assumed that you had something to bring to the party. Something more than this pitiful little thing. Nestor, look at this little pee-pee."

Nestor began to chuckle, compared to this young punk, he seemed like a stallion.

"Hey, that's not cool. You didn't even give me a chance."

"A chance for what?" said Lupe. "A chance to go find the rest of your cock?"

"I thought size wasn't supposed to matter." said the driver.

"Maybe size doesn't matter." she said as she looked at Nestor to reassure him. "But what you've got there doesn't qualify as a size."

"This is so fucked." said the driver.

"This was all your idea, *pindejo*." she said. "Look, put your little golf pencil away, get back in the front seat, roll the screen up and drive this fucking car to the hotel. Now go, *vamanos*."

Lupe looked out the window with a warm, glowing smile as she calmly reclined against her husband, sipping complimentary champagne. She admitted to herself that although she didn't understand it yet, something had changed between them, this trip could turn out well after all.

Nestor felt a unfamiliar warmth and savored the first genuinely precious moment of their marriage, finally affection seemed possible between them. He was content to sit back and bask in it. Surely, this too, would pass.

Aztlánicon
Only To Bring Forth Thistles And Thorns

Poco despues, the limo pulled up to the Hotel Tamaulipas; the bell captain opened the rear door. Nestor stepped from the car and turned to offer his hand. Guadalupe stepped from the car. As usual, heads turned to look at her. With the door still ajar, the limo suddenly sped off, the door struck a parked car as it went around the corner.

"Our luggage is still in there. I need my luggage." said Nestor.

"I'm sorry about this. He's kind of a pampered asshole. Why don't we get you and your companion checked in, I'll radio the kid to come back here with your luggage and we'll get it up to your room right away."

Going up in the elevator, Nestor watched the young bellhop fondle Lupe with his eyes, he could tell how she enjoyed it, even though she pretended not to. Nestor knew exactly why the bellhop trailed several paces behind them. Lupe gladly provided something to look at. Nestor wondered if this was what would make her happy. It might be worth it to try out something.

The bags had yet to be recovered from the runaway limo, but the bellhop still presented himself for the customary tipping moment. Nestor's blood boiled as he hung on the precipice. Should he do this? Should he not? Finally, he decided.

"You know, I see you looking at my companion in a certain way. Do you want to fuck her?"

Stunned, the bellhop said, " No, *Señor*."

"Nestor, What are you doing?" said Lupe. She looked at the young man in disbelief. "Wait one minute. You're saying that you don't want to fuck me? You expect us to believe that bullshit? You're gonna stand there and insult me. Do you know who this man is?"

The confused bellhop capitulated, "Okay, I admit I do want to fuck her."

"What are you waiting for?" said Nestor as he pushed the young man toward Lupe.

Lupe studied Nestor to sense why he was doing this. As the young man stumbled toward her, she decided to go along with it. She turned around and rubbed against the young man, checking with Nestor every few moments. She could feel the bell-hop trace his bulge on her ass, his hands came around and cupped her breasts, Lupe looked right into Nestor's eyes, -- Is this what you want?

The bell-hop reached under Lupe's blouse and began to feel her warm brown skin, his fingers lightly pinched her dark nipples through her bra, as he ground into her from behind. Lupe reached down and unzipped the bell-hop, she reached inside his pants and pulled out his penis. There was no complaint. She knelt down and began to felate him while Nestor stood by and watched.

"Enough!" said Nestor. He rushed over and pushed the bellhop down, "I said that's enough!"

The young man just laid on the floor gasping. He got up and adjusted his organ back to where it came from. He looked at them like they were crazy. He headed for the door and closed it behind him.

Lupe reclined on the sofa in complete amazement.

"Nestor Salamanca, what the hell has gotten into you?"

"I don't know. I couldn't go through with it. I couldn't stand watching you on your knees with anyone but me."

They sat in silence for a few moments and Nestor finally spoke.

Aztlánicon
Only To Bring Forth Thistles And Thorns

"So what do you want now?"

"I'm kind of in the mood now, what do you think?"

"I want you so bad right now."

Nestor helped Lupe to her feet and they kissed passionately. He carried her to the bedroom where they coupled like wild animals.

Nestor puffed on a Cuban cigar and took in the sunset from the south facing balcony, basking in the glow of the best sex of his life. But how could it go on like this? This was crazy.

Lupe stood at the doorway in a robe that partially concealed her body, "Let's go dancing. Or are you going to keep me imprisoned in this room?"

"I'm not sure."

"I'm going to go insane if I'm cooped up."

"This is the Presidential Suite, probably the best hotel room in this part of Mexico, and still you're not content. What the hell do you want from me?"

"I told you, I've already got what I wanted from you."

"Then why do you give me grief?"

"I don't want to be taken for granted."

"Since when do I take you for granted?"

"If it's easy for you, then you won't appreciate me. What's the use of being beautiful if you aren't coveted."

"I desire you. You're the most beautiful woman I've ever seen."

"I'm used to that, but that feeling of that bellboy drinking me up with his eyes, and his hands needing to caress my body, despite it all being so awkward with you there."

"Is that what you want, to have sex with other men?"

"It was enough to know that he wanted me. It's way more fun to deny them then to let them have their way."

Nestor smiled.

That Which Hath Been Subject To Ancient Dispute

2015
Nuevo Laredo, Mexico

The following morning, in the dimness of the *Presidente* suite, Nestor Salamanca stood over his sleeping Lupe and acknowledged that this woman's location would always be his domicile, the place to which he would always intend to return.

He leaned down and adjusted the sheet that almost concealed her. He nuzzled the back of her neck, taking in the aroma of her hair. He lightly kissed her cheek, as his hand gently caressed her flesh. For a few precious moments nothing else existed but this beautiful woman; not the *coyote* business, the return from exile or anything like that. When the phone rang the state of being collapsed. Lupe stirred. Nestor quickly grabbed the instrument before it could ring again.

"Yes?"

"Sorry to disturb you sir, but the car is here." said the voice on the phone.

"All right, I'll be right down." he said as he reached over and gently returned the telephone to its cradle.

Lupe slowly turned over and faced him.

"It's still dark outside?" she said.

"No, the drapes are closed."

"What time is it?"

"It's time for me to go."

"Do you have to? This trip is starting to be fun."

"Business is business, *mi amor*. I'll be back later and we'll pick up where we left off."

For his benefit she dreamily closed her eyes and said, "I'll be waiting for you."

"Lupe, please stay in the hotel complex. It's dangerous for you."

"I was just going to do a little shopping. I can blend in."

"Kidnappers get unemployment insurance down here. It's a way of life. A beautiful *pocha* like you? Out there you're going to stick out like free lunch. Consider how much fun they'll have while they wait for me to come up with the ransom."

Lupe hadn't thought of that.

"They have shops right here in the hotel complex. Please do me a favor and stay in the hotel."

"Maybe I'll just lay out in the sun."

"Use the balcony and please not in the nude. Enough people see you in the nude."

She smirked at him. Nestor knew that she'd lay out in the nude no matter what he said. He leaned over and kissed her. As he stood up, his eyes lingered on her exquisite form. He gently traced his index finger along her generous rear for the last time.

"Maybe I should go with you." she said.

"No, you sleep. I'll be fine. I'll see you later this

evening. We'll have some more fun tonight, before we go home tomorrow." He turned and walked across the room.

Lupe watched him in the dimness as he opened the door and was lit by the sunlight spilling in from the next room. He turned toward her with a bashful, submissive look on his face that was unattractive to her.

"I'll be thinking of coming back to you the whole time." he said.

Lupe bristled and bolted upright in anger.

"That's what I'm afraid of. You'd better pay attention to what you're doing, *pindejo*. This is a big day. You're supposed to be bringing the *familia* back from exile, not thinking about sex games with your wife."

"I don't really care about coming back from exile. In fact, fuck the *Ayunta*. Mama saved the *familia* and we've gotten along the way things are. We'll just carry on in my mother's way."

"Nestor. You are not your mother. God rest her soul."

"I know that. You don't think I'm strong enough to take over for my mother. You're like the rest of them."

"That's it. I'm going with you. I'm not going to let you fuck this up." she said as she flung aside the sheet and got up.

"Bullshit. I'm not bringing my wife to a summit. It's like you said back home. I'd never live it down. I'll listen to what they have to say. Then I'll come back here to you."

"*Derota*. With this attitude you'll be lucky to come back at all."

"Thanks for the support." said Nestor as he closed

the door.

As Lupe layed awake in the darkness, she heard the outer door close and suddenly the room was silent. She breathed slowly and deeply to neutralize the bad images she had of Nestor. Eventually, the disturbing thoughts settled, but, she would never get back to sleep. She collected herself enough to order breakfast. After hanging up she layed back and thought about how unnecessary the warning was. She had no desire to go outside and mingle with the denizens of Nuevo Laredo.

Outside town, the car bearing Nestor Salamanca drove up to the guard gate at Paco Izqueirdo's estate. The car was immediately set upon by two agents with barely controllable dogs that disappeared under the car, Nestor noticed the *gringo* emblems on the uniforms.

"Paco Izqueirdo has his own car searched with dogs? Is it always like this?"

"Sorry about this, sir. There's new people that suddenly seem to matter. This was all their idea."

Nestor saw a third agent sweep the car with a tiny video camera on the end of a telescoping pole. A forth agent intently studied a handheld video monitor. After the dogs searched the trunk, the rear door opened and one of the dogs jumped into the compartment and went over everything inside the car with his snout, including Nestor.

"Please step out of the car sir." said the *gringo* agent.

Nestor managed his offendedness and stepped from the car where he was instructed to raise his arms and was scanned. Finding nothing, the agent instructed him to return to his seat.

As the car pulled up to the front of the *hacienda* the door was flung open by another *gringo* agent with an automatic weapon slung over the shoulder. As the agent stepped aside Nestor saw one of Izquierdo's stewards, the first friendly face since his arrival.

"*Don* Salamanca, please come with me, the swarm has already begun."

Nestor followed the steward and noticed the obvious changes to Izqueirdo's estate since the last time. There were always guards, but never so governmental. No one outside of government ever enjoyed having uniforms around.

Along the way, Nestor took in the splendor of the huge dwelling, an elegant blend of ancient and postmodern, adobe and glass used in an other-worldly manner, as if eco-Hobbits had built it on some space-opera planet. Nestor admired the smooth flowing adobe walls that angled down at the perimeter and blended into the landscape on either side of the enormous 21st century earthship. He was led out into the lush hanging gardens of the courtyard. The *bellasombre* trees were more developed and provided large zones of welcoming shade so that various rivals could flock with their brethren and spare themselves the discomfort of making nice with a mortal enemy.

Nestor strolled around the courtyard unnoticed as the *coyotes* mingled in the tight murmur of brutish chit-chat He was a newcomer to most of these people, which was fine with him. The faint balm of jasmine, sage and acacia, were gradually eclipsed by the pall of Cuban cigars.

As Paco Izqueirdo emerged from the earthship *hacienda*, the underworld chit-chat died out immediately. Izqueirdo was accompanied by the titans of human smuggling in the Americas, Manuel Matanza and next to him Gasparo Feodora, the elder statesman. There were others that Nestor didn't recognize.

Izqueirdo took a *Partaga* from a cigar box and leaned over to have it lit, he then took a *cuba libre*.

"Gentlemen. Would you please find your seats, your names are on the little place cards at each table. Please sit in your assigned seats." said Izqueirdo.

The *coyotes* milled around for a moment, unsure of what to do.

"*Don* Izqueirdo--- We can't just sit with our own people, like always?" said someone from the crowd.

"Gentlemen, the phrase 'like always' no longer applies. Forget that you even know it. Today we begin a new era in the human smuggling trade. Today marks the death of business as usual." said *Don* Izqueirdo.

Nestor didn't like the sound of that, but still he joined in with everyone else in finding their placecard. His was at a table near the podium. The placecard to the left of his read *Don* Feodora and the one to the right, *Don* Matanza. What in the hell was going on? He'd been assigned to sit between two of the most powerful players at the *honcho* table?

Suddenly, he was staggered in the way it feels prior to vomiting, the way your mouth fills with saliva. To calm himself, he rationalized that this was probably some gesture extended to welcome him back from exile. There was no reason to be concerned, at least, that's how he rationalized the situation to console himself. He could just relax and eat a nice meal, get a little buzzed and then go back to the hotel and Lupe.

When Gasparo Feodora took his seat, Nestor hardly noticed. He was holding his drink in one hand and the cigar in the other and only managed to insinuate rising and a clumsy nod. The old man was obviously not impressed. Realizing that he'd muffed it, Nestor set down the glass and carefully balanced the burning cigar on top of it. He then stood properly and turned toward *Don* Feodora.

"Excuse me *señor*, that was no way to greet a man of your stature, please forgive me." said Nestor as he extended his hand.

The damage had already been done, the old man barely extended his arm in greeting. Nestor limply took the *anciano's* hand and managed a handshake as best he could.

"On behalf of *Familia* Salamanca, I wish to thank you for allowing us back."

"It was the ruling of the *Ayutamiento*, not me. Besides, you're not 'back in' just yet." said Feodora.

"Well, sir, to whatever degree my *familia* has been restored, I know you must have influenced it. My father used to say, 'Always keep in mind that *La Tuberias* operates only with Gasparo Feodora's blessing. If we lose that, we're done."

"That was your father. Your *familia* operated for years outside our blessing." said Feodora.

"Only with great difficulty, *señor*."

"Well, things should get better now that your mother is gone." said the *anciano*. "We all thought very highly of her. It broke our hearts to have her killed."

"The *Ayunta* had her killed?"

"We had no choice. No matter how highly we thought of her, she was a woman. We can't have a *familia* headed by a woman. It's bad for business." said Feodora.

"So then what required having her killed?" said Nestor.

"*La Tuberias* didn't flounder, like it was supposed to. Rosalie Salamanca was too resourceful for anyone's good." said Feodora with a slight smile. "She was warned about this, but she stubbornly refused to remarry."

"So, the *Ayuntamiento* was threatened by her success in exile?" said Nestor.

"Thank you for coming. *Salud*." said Izqueirdo to the gathering, as he lifted his glass.

En masse, the *coyotes* lifted their glasses and joined in, "*Salud*."

"May I present our diplomatic genius, Javier Enalda-Calderon." said Izqueirdo.

Enalda-Calderon stood from across the table and waved amid the gracious applause.

"He's the one who hammered out the understanding between the *Quetzaltepeques* and the *Frontera Candaleria* gang. Look they've been sitting at the same table for five minutes now with no shots fired."

Nestor tried his best to follow along with the social niceties, but his head pounded with rage in the wake of what Feodora said about his mother.

"All of this recent violence only proves that we need to make some changes." said Izquierdo. "We've operated independently up until now and we've been fortunate enough to have had things our own way, but that is all about to change."

"Because of globalization and the so-called free trade." said one of the coyotes.

"Our whole world has been taken over by these *pinche* corporations." said another.

"And they're leaving no room for honest *coyotes* to make a living."

"These fucking newcomers are giving us bad reputations." said Enalda-Calderon.

"When did we ever have good reputations?" said

Aztlánicon
That Which Hath Been Subject To Ancient Dispute

Feodora.

It was then that someone no one knew stood up at the *honcho* table.

"Gentlemen, human smuggling has joined drugs and gun running as a top global enterprise." said the man that no one knew. He was a *euro-gringo*, not one of the *coyotes*.

"In other words, there's too much fucking money in it for us to keep it to ourselves." interjected Izqueirdo.

"I heard that one of these newcomers charges extra for taking people all the way to Los Angeles and then dumps them off in Los Angeles, Texas." said one of the *Frontera Candaleria* gang

"At least they were still alive. Some of these *pinche* intruders just take the money and leave the people to roast to death in the back of a truck." said Guillermo Montoya.

"Yeah, it's not like running drugs." said one of the *Quetzaltepeques*. "When they've already been paid it's too easy for these *pindejos* to just walk away from a truckload of dying people. They'd never just walk away from a truckload of cocaine."

"I think the point is, gentlemen, you no longer have the *coyote* trade to yourselves." said the *euro-gringo*. "You're now facing competition with the Chinese Triads, the Yakuzas, even the Albanian Mafia. The smuggling of humans is now big business and the *pinche* corporations, as you call them, are most definately going to take over."

"*Amigos*, this gentleman is the reason I've asked you here." said Paco Izqueirdo. "May I introduce *señor* Manfred Brandt, who is with the WTO and he has a proposition for us."

"Gentlemen, the Free Trade Area of the Americas is here and the era of free trade is upon us and government monopolies are over."said Brandt. "But, there is some good news. The organizations that I represent are going to allow you to continue to operate. Some new rules, of course. From now on you'll be sub-contracting for us."

Nestor had heard enough.

"Wait a minute, you're going to *allow* us to operate?" said Nestor. He looked to the others for support, he found none. "What about the re-conquest of *Aztlan*?"

"What about it?" said Montoya.

"Some of us have been involved with it for many years now. said Nestor. "Don't we have a duty to the *la raza*? Are we just going to let these *gringos* and their *pinche* corporations come in and take over?"

"Salamanca, you're the only one worried about that shit." said Paco Izqueirdo. "Grow up, would you?"

"Mister Salamanca, the re-conquest of *Aztlan* is moot at this point."said Brandt. "All of that tired *reconquista* shit has outlived it's usefullness. There is a new world order in operation and if you can't fit in with that, perhaps you should move to Cuba."

"You're going along with this?" said Nestor to all of those assembled.

Except for the locusts, there was silence in the courtyard.

Nestor realized that the *coyotes* weren't even going to so much as pout about the *Euro-gringo* takeover. He stood for a moment and finished the *cuba libre*. He dabbed his mouth with a very nice paper napkin, which he stuffed into the glass, which he set down on the *honcho* table. He then dropped the burning cigar into the glass and walked out. A small glass fire ensued.

Aztlánicon
That Which Hath Been Subject To Ancient Dispute

It was a very somber drive back to Nuevo Laredo. Nestor ruminated over his questionalble future. He wondered how to salvage his business on his own. He knew he'd acted impulsively. He'd give himself tonight to cool off and maybe patch things up in the morning. Thank God, Lupe was at the hotel and he could get his mind off of things.

Aztlanicon:
CODEX V

Oblige Thy God Through Labyrinths Of Vice

2015
Nuevo Laredo,
Estados Unitos de Mexico

3 THE EYES OF THE LORD ARE EVERYWHERE, IN EVERY
PLACE, BEHOLDING THE EVIL AND THE GOOD.
--- PROVERBS 15

That evening, three years into the age of *Itza*, Nestor
Salamanca was hopelessly distracted over ruining his
familia's return from exile. He poured another glass of
Respiro in the *El Presidente* suite of Hotel Tamaulipas.
Away from the machismo puffery he'd displayed at the
coyote summit, it was obvious that instead of delivering
his *familia* from exile, he'd made things even worse with
the *Ayunta*. The usually familiar tequila suddenly seemed
the flavor of desperation.

Even in the midst of melancholic self-medication his
mind floundered bitterly over what should have been
done. His Mother's voice trickled in from the past to
haunt him, "Nestor, your mind never occupies the same
space as your molecules. You must learn to be present."
Only one thing in this universe had the power to get
Nestor's mind out of the tortured past and into the
present moment. She was getting ready in the next
room.

Nestor sat back into the voluptuous leather sofa, the
kind you would only find on that side of the river. He
sipped some more tequila and wondered what was
keeping her? When she's in the room it's impossible to
think of anything else. He needed that right now.

Nestor never wanted the role of *Don*, at least until he discovered Lupe Obregon. If Nestor hadn't been the *heir apparent*, Lupe would have never been interested in someone like him. Because of his flagrant disinterest in the *familia*, Nestor always presumed that Eberto would be the one to take things over, but that was when he still believed Eberto to be a Salamanca, before the *Doña* revealed that her younger son was someone else's bastard.

Nestor's ascension to *Don* didn't involve clawing his way through the vicious food chain. Nothing like it. Nestor inherited *familia* Salamanca like an heirloom tea set that he didn't really know what to do with. Nestor would have been perfectly content to let Eberto run things if the *Doña* hadn't sworn to *Don* Emiliano that the son of Rudolpho Aguirre would never be the head of *familia* Salamanca.

While he waited impatiently, Nestor set down the half empty glass and removed from his pocket the little mirror that he got at the *place of miracles* two days earlier. The mirror that lulled him into that foolish prayer. Nestor lightly fingered the *Virgen's* silk-screened image on the back of the mirror. He became increasingly more sensitive to the image's relief, lulled into that strange feeling, just like a few days earlier at Painted Pony Park. He remembered reflecting the sunbeam on the *milagro* and the feeling that overcame him, the feeling that he must have imagined, at least, that's how he felt at the time. Nestor was inexplicably moved to pray.

"Holy *Virgen*, you must know that I don't really believe in you. But, I'm going to ask for your help anyway, just in case. Holy *Virgen*, please help me to shed all the bullshit of being the *Don* and let me just spend what's left of my life with my Lupe." he said as he imagined the prayer going to the *Virgen*, like his mother taught him. Nestor sat quietly, in meditative silence, like his mother taught him.

There was a knock at the door.

Aztlanicon:
CODEX V

"Who is it?"

"Tijereta."

Nestor thought it odd that one of Paco Izqueirdo's lieutenants would come calling this late. Nestor leaned over and peeped through the lens in the door. It was Tijereta alright. What the hell does he want? Nestor momentarily considered not opening the door, but, it was Paco Izqueirdo's hotel and Tijereta was the hotel manager. If they want to get in, they will. Reluctant, he opened the door.

"I'm calling Izqueirdo in the morning to square it with him and the *Ayunta*." said Nestor.

As the door opened fully, a large Mexican hoodlum pointed a gun and motioned Nestor to step back. Nestor did so. The hoodlum stepped aside and Tijereta entered. For an underworld functionary, Tijereta created a dapper impression via his proud carriage.

"Paco Izqueirdo and the *Ayunta* were very dissappointed at the display you put on today." said Tijereta.

"I was just doing what I thought was best for *mi familia*."

"And the *Ayunta* is just doing what's best for everyone. This globalization bullshit is fucking everything up for everybody."

"I realize that now, but I'll get it together. I swear it."

"It's too late for that. Other arrangements have been made. Arrangements you are not a part of." said Tijereta as he looked toward the door. "Luiz, come in here."

In through the door stepped the timid figure, Nestor was so shaken that he didn't even notice who it was.

Aztlanicon
Oblige Thy God Through Labyrinths Of Vice

"This is my nephew. You have the honor of popping his cherry." said Tijereta as he motioned toward the youth. "Come on over here."

As the nephew stepped closer, Nestor saw that it was the brash young limo driver Lupe humiliated two days before.

"Remember me?"

"Oh, do you two know each other?" said Tijereta.

"Not really, I drove them from the airport. Why should he remember me?"

"Well, that makes it a little more interesting." said Tijereta. "Get on with it."

The nephew looked at his uncle, "Are you going to watch?"

"Planned on it." said Tijereta.

"I wanted to have some fun with him first."

"Not a good idea." said Tijereta.

"Please, uncle. Please?"

Tijereta looked at Nestor and shrugged his shoulders, "My sister's boy, what are you going to do? I've spoiled the little pervert."

Tijereta motioned to the large thug to give the gun to the nephew, the thug then left the room and Tijereta followed. As he reached the door, Tijereta turned and said to his sister's boy, "Don't take too long, and don't make a mess. I'll be down in the bar. We'll have *mojitos* to celebrate. Today you are a man,... sort of."

Tijereta closed the door behind him. The nephew pointed the gun at Nestor, "Get on your knees."

Aztlanicon:
CODEX V

Nestor did as ordered, the nephew fumbled with his zipper and pulled out his penis. He grabbed Nestor by the hair and dangled the tiny thing next to him.

"Let's see if it's too small. If you still feel like laughing." said the nephew.

∴ Ω ∴

In the adjacent dressing room, Lupe gently ground her pelvis against the counter to warm herself up. With lipstick even more red than the dress she'd purchased that afternoon, she painted her version of a prostitute across her beautiful face. She wanted tonight to be even more combustible than the night before. She had to find a way of making this marriage of convenience, more convenient; or else it would never last.

As she pulled down her panties and sat down to pee, she imagined the strange men, as they would dance in the dimness, as their hands would trace the opulent curves of her body, as Nestor would watch them handle his trophy.

As she finished, she heard talking in the main room, the voices were drowned out by the flushing toilet. Nestor must have sent for room service. Perhaps tonight will start off with the room-service guy. It'll be fun, maybe it will even get Nestor out of his funk. "Hey, mister, what's it gonna be? A fuck or a suck?" she said playfully as the door opened. Lupe entered the main room to find the nephew holding a gun to Nestor's head, Nestor could have been blowing him, it was hard to tell.

"Nestor, what the hell is going on?" she said.

Nestor pulled away as the nephew turned toward Lupe.

"Well, hello." said the nephew. "God, if you're not the most beautiful bitch I've ever seen."

Nestor quickly reached up and tried to grab the

nephew by the balls, there wasn't much to grab.

He struck Nestor in the head with the gun,"Fuck you."

Nestor slumped over and held his head.

"Well, then, everybody's here. So, let's finish the party we started the other day." said the nephew as he again pointed the gun at Nestor's forehead.

Nestor Salamanca was oddly content to spend the final moments of his life looking at Lupe. He silently mouthed 'I love you'.

The nephew grew weary of Nestor and pulled the trigger. The exit wound was massive, messy. Blood and brains splattered onto the carpet, onto the lower portion of wall. Nestor's lifeless body collapsed onto the floor. Lupe gasped.

The nephew turned to her, "Enough with him. Now I can focus on you. So, did you miss me? Did you miss laughing at me, and my little friend here?

He stuck out his tiny penis, still wet with saliva. At least that question was answered. The nephew sat on the large leather sofa.

"What was it you said when you came in? What's it gonna be? A fuck or a suck? Well, I don't really have time for a fuck, I'm supposed to go have drinks with my uncle. Let's see if you can suck better than the late Nestor Salamanca. Or is my little dick too funny?"

Lupe looked at the gun, at his tiny penis, at her husband's corpse.

"What the fuck are you looking at him for? He can't help you now."

The nephew turned and fired another bullet into the lifeless corpse and said, "You don't think my dick is funny anymore, do you?"He turned back to Lupe.

"So, do you want to suck it, or is it too funny?"

"Let me put a condom on you first." she said.

"Fuck that. What's the point with those things, they don't work, they always slide right off."

Lupe desperately fought the dark impulse to snicker.

"Besides, you won't have to worry about getting anything." he smiled to reassure her. "Look, you do this like you mean it, without laughing, and I'll let you walk out of here alive. That's fair, right?"

In the most matter of fact manner possible, Lupe slowly dropped to her knees and took the minute member into her mouth for the second time in as many days. He closed his eyes and moaned as his head tilted back.

"That's it. Do it just like that." he said, as his moaning increased, "We're almost there."

Lupe knew that no matter what this *putamadre* said, he wasn't going to let her live and there was no way that the final few moments of her life were going to be spent sucking off this little weasel.

He put the gun to her head. "You're gonna swallow it, beautiful bitch. We'll see who's laughing."

Lupe knew it was now or never, she bit down as hard as she could on the little penis. The nephew screamed as he swiped at her head.

"Agggghhhh. Let go." he yelled, as he again swung at her.

Lupe stood as much as she could with his dick between her teeth. Like a shark, she viciously jerked from side to side until the little penis ripped off and blood started gushing out. Suddenly dickless, the nephew dropped the gun and put both hands where the penis used to be. The blood intended to make the little appendage hard was now gushing onto the sofa and carpet.

Lupe grabbed the gun and stood triumphant. She looked at the squirming nephew and spat out the penis onto the bed.

"Yuck." she said as she wiped her mouth with her arm.

"Help me."

"So what do you think? Was I better than Nestor?"

"Help me!"

"Oh, I'll help you, alright. Scoot back there."

The pervert nephew offered no resistance. How could he? He looked at the beautiful *pocha* holding the gun on him and wondered how it came to this. He inched back on the blood soaked sofa toward the mirrored wall. Weaker and weaker, he leaned back against the wall with hope fading that she would take any sort of pity as his precious five liters continued to gush.

"You know what I just realized." she said, "It's really dangerous to have a mirror next to where you sleep. What if there's an earthquake?"

"Please help me. I'm so cold."

"Your pain will be over soon. Who sent you to kill my husband?"

"Your husband? He said you two weren't married."

"He lied. He was such a fucking liar sometimes."

"Please help me."

"You know, I'm no doctor, but you seem to be bleeding pretty bad. Why don't you tell me who sent you and I'll send for help."

"My Uncle Tijereta."

"What's your uncle have against my husband?"

"I don't know," he gasped, "Something about the *Ayunta*."

Lupe figured that she had gotten as much out of him as he had left to give, "Now sit back. That's good, now, go 'ooohhh' with your mouth,"she said as she puckered her lips.

"You're not sending for help are you?"

"Come on. Haven't you ever gone to the movies? Of course, I'm not sending for help. Now, go 'ooohhh' with your mouth."

"Fuck you."

It occured to Lupe that she had never actually fired a gun before. She'd never bitten off a penis before either. How hard could it be? Lupe gathered all the rage and ancestral horror that inhabited the blood of the Obregon women and she focused it into the bullet that patiently waited in the chamber. She stuck the gun in his mouth and pulled the trigger. The bullet exploded through the *medulla oblagata* and shattered the huge mirror behind him.

$$\therefore \Omega \therefore$$

Poco despues, Lupe paced the room drenched in the energy of bloodlust, she looked for something else to put a bullet into, she glanced at Nestor's corpse and put another bullet in him.

"That's for messing around with sex games while you should have been taking care of your business. You fucking *derota*."

Lupe paced around more, she wondered what in the hell she was going to do next. She knew that she couldn't let herself fall apart right now. She looked at the dead nephew and noticed chunks of broken glass had cut into his shoulders and thighs.

"See what I mean about mirrors? They're dangerous."

Lupe stepped back to assess her handywork. The sofa was covered in the nephew's congealed blood. The facial half of the skull remained mostly intact, tilted backward and to the right.The tiny penis that Lupe bit off earlier, now barely stuck out of the corpse's mouth. She reached over to pull it out just a little further, it fell onto the lap, very near it's original location.

"*Putamadre!*"

She picked up the penis and replaced it in the corpse's mouth, she tilted what was left of the head back further and closed the mouth down on it.

"There."

Tiny bits of brain and blood were fanned out like a grotesque tie-dye pattern on the wall behind him. She'd written in the blood:

Sacapuntas

She carefully drew an arrow down to the dead mouth, bent the bloodied cotton swab in half and walked into the bathroom and tossed it into the toilet. She stared into the mirror and was stunned at what a hideous, bloody mess she was.

"Luiz?... What the fuck's keeping you man?" said a voice coming from the front door. Tijereta's hoodlum cautiously wandered into the suite.

"Luiz? Stop messing around."

The hoodlum stopped in his tracks when he saw the nephew laying against the bloddy wall. How could Luiz have fucked this up? All he had to do was shoot one *pinche* looser from *Califas*. How hard could that be? While the hoodlum stood and wondered how Luiz could have fucked this up, he had no idea of how much he had fucked up. It didn't dawn on him that he'd left the door open until a *gringo* lady passing in the hallway, poked her head inside to glimpse the *El Presidente* suite. It was her screaming down the hallway that undid everything.

Lupe heard the screaming and knew that it was the appropriate time to leave. She slipped out through the glass door onto the balcony and looked around for an escape. The only way was down. The suite stuck out from the rest of the building and it was an intimidating distance down to the next balcony. Lupe hung over the side with the intention of getting to the balcony below, but it was too far.

The hoodlum had re-entered the suite from the hallway with his handgun drawn. In his haste he knocked over a lamp.

Lupe heard the noise from the next room and crept over the balcony railing. She knew she was running out of time. She looked down at the balcony below. It was so far away. She glanced down at the pool below. It was even further away, but making it to the pool seemed more do-able than the balcony below. She heard another noise and knew it was time to decide.

"Fuck it." she said as she closed her eyes, leaned out and took the plunge.

$$\therefore \Omega \therefore$$

Gun first, the hoodlum cautiously inched his way toward the glass door that opened onto the balcony. He slowly brushed aside the curtains and peeked outside, first to the left, then to the right. There was no one there.

He holstered his weapon and stepped onto the balcony to get some air. He stood there and gazed upon the lights of Nuevo Laredo and across the river to Laredo, Texas. As he wondered what he was going to tell Tijereta, his eyes drifted down below toward the pool. The lights were on and the water was red,... blood red.

∴ Ω ∴

Poco despues, back in the *Presidente* Suite, Antonio Tijereta resented that the officers of the Nuevo Laredo Police were so amused by the grotesque misfortune of his nephew. He bitterly resented the show a certain *pendejo* police detective was putting on with his cellphone/camera, fussing around to get just the right framing of his nephew's body, his little severed penis slightly sticking from his mouth, above him, the word *sacapuntas* written in blood on the wall and an arrow drawn down to the nephew's head. Above all of it, in blood, is written,

Deuteronomy 23: 2

"Do we know what Deuteronomy twenty-three verse two says?" said *Policia* Inspector Gomez.

"We sent someone for a Bible sir." said the junior detective.

Shocked, Gomez turned to Tijereta.

"What? There are no Bibles in the rooms here at Hotel Tamaulipas?" said Gomez.

A uniformed officer entered the room with a Catholic Bible and the junior detective took it and opened the book to the passage indicated in the blood.

"Here it is sir, No one whose testicles have been crushed or whose penis has been cut off, may be admitted into the community of the LORD."

"Whoever did this is very clever."

"And quite vengeful." said *Policia* Inspector Gomez. "It makes the Tamaulipas syndicate look pretty damned impotent. And right here on your own turf."

Tijereta stood unresponsive.

"Tijereta, isn't this poor fool a realtive of yours?" said Inspector Gomez, knowing full well that that was the case.

"My sister's boy."

"Well, from now on, if he's remembered at all, he's going to be remembered as the pencil sharpener."

"I hope for your wife's sake that tiny cocks aren't a family trait." said a uniform cop. "If they are, tell her I'll come over and help her out."

"I think he'll be fine with the LORD." said the junior detective. "Yes, it was severed, but, that doesn't qualify as a penis."

Several officers in the room laughed. Tijereta noted every one of them. Somehow, each of these *putamadres* would pay for this humiliation.

Policia Inspector Gomez looked at Nestor's corpse crumpled in the corner. "Who's this over here and why was he spared the *sacapuntas* treatment?"

"I don't know much about him. A businessman from California. Involved in imports, I think." said Tijereta.

"Imports,... of course. Was he alone?"

"I believe the register shows a companion." said Tijereta.

"You're going to have to do better than that. Male? Female? Canine?"

There was more laughter in the room.

Tijereta did not find any of this amusing. "Female." he said.

"Is there a name?"

"She was registered under the name, Guadalupe Obregon. Also, from California."

"Where is she now?" said Gomez.

"I have no idea."

"Tijereta. What kind of show you putting on here?"

"I beg your pardon?"

"This kind of shit makes all of Tamaulipas look bad, like we're barbaric or something. It's bad enough we're trying to survive this fucking NAFTA economy."

"Inspector, I certainly don't enjoy the fact that these people were murdered on my watch. Especially when one of them is a blood relative. I don't enjoy the fact that our best suite has been turned into a fucking slaughterhouse. This all makes me look bad."

"But, worse, it makes Paco Izqueirdo look bad." said Gomez.

"And that means that you could be the next one to wind up with your dick in your mouth." said Gomez.

As Tijereta left the room, he felt shame for the helplessness of his circumstances, he could only stand and watch the police parade through his suite, as they came to see for themselves the hilarious crime scene.

Aztlanicon:
CODEX V

Whoever did this must pay. Paco Izqueirdo was going to demand that it be settled in the most public, humiliating way possible. No one can embarrass *Tamaulipas* like this. Whoever did this is dead. Not simply dead, but ceremoniously dead,... with pomp and circumstance.

$$\therefore \Omega \therefore$$

Dripping wet, Lupe toweled herself off in a service stairwell and changed into a housekeeping uniform found in a utility closet. She was only approximately conscious of how different her life had become in the last sixty minutes.

A stairwell door opened several floors above.

"Search these stairs all the way down." said a voice, echoing down the shaft.

Lupe knew that if she was going to survive the night, she had to get out of there right now. She peered through a small window into the lobby. The coast wasn't exactly clear, but it was clear enough. Lupe cautiously slipped out into the foreign, hostile night.

Cast Unto This Veil Of Misery

2015
Nuevo Laredo, Mexico

THERE IS NOTHING SO WRETCHED OR FOOLISH AS TO
ANTICIPATE MISFORTUNES. WHAT MADNESS IT IS IN
EXPECTING EVIL BEFORE IT ARRIVES.

--- SENECA

As she grasped at the faint trails of her freshly vanquished life, Lupe wandered the unfamiliar streets of Nuevo Laredo and struggled to avoid the near certain descent into the viscous foodchain of the borderland. She'd already been offered money twice that morning for sex. One was a fat-ass *gringo* across the border for the day. She never considered it with him for even a moment. The other was a street-boy *entrepreneur* who claimed to have some manner of porn website. Despite her weakness for bad boys, Lupe was indignant at the proposition and told him to go away. But, her hunger had become so oppressive, that if he appeared again and propositioned her at that very moment, she would consider it very seriously.

As she plodded along the street in her bare feet, Lupe spotted a bench in the buzy plaza across from a church. She needed to rest and it seemed a good place to do so. She collapsed on the bench and glanced around to get her bearings. Just a few blocks away was the Hotel Tamaulipas and the balcony where just the day before she'd laid out in the nude. The same balcony she jumped from hours later. Her ribs were still tender from the not so perfect entry angle into the pool.

People had gathered across the street, in the lot behind the old church. Lupe moved toward them to see what was going on. It was a welcome sight to see that food was being served to what appeared to be needy locals and destitute pilgrims. She'd qualify. You couldn't get more destitute then she was.

Lupe waited at the end of the food line. With plenty of time to look around, she noticed that against the wall there was a freebox of clothes. She jumped out of line and rummaged through the creepy pile. Most of the clothes were the cast-offs of meso-Americans on the long dangerous journey north. You could imagine the selection. Lupe, sorted wantonly through the large box, desperate to shed the housekeeping look she had on. Suddenly she detected the aroma of her perfume. She dug further into the box. There were some of her clothes. She pulled them out and held them wadded together against her nose. For a brief moment the aroma made her feel almost normal, but not for long. Off to the side was one of the bags she'd left behind in the suite. She grabbed it and stuffed her clothes inside. While she looked around for a place to change, she noticed a young local woman wearing the red dress she'd bought in the hotel the day before. She was bitter to give up that dress, especially when she looked so much better in it than this local *puta*. But she was in the middle of all the trouble she could handle at the moment and decided to let it pass.

Poco déspues, Lupe emerged from the church restroom with the suitcase towed behind. She wore the most practical outfit she could put together from her clothes she found in the freebox, but she still had no shoes. Back at the freebox, she could only find a pair of worn-out *hurache* sandals. She cringed at the thought of the feet that had been in these sandals previously. But, her feet were killing her and the disgusting *huraches* would have to fill the bill for now.

Nearby the church restroom, an office door opened and out walked a weathered *gringo* wearing clothes that would pass as a common local. He looked at Lupe and tipped his hat. She somehow felt drawn to him, not in a sexual way, but there was a mysterious attraction that existed on another level.

"Was it okay I took these sandals?"

"That's what they're there for." said the *gringo*, he nodded and walked toward a donkey cart filled with supplies. He grabbed hold of the reins, gently patted the donkey's hindquarters and climbed into the seat. Lupe cautiously approached.

"Excuse me Could you help me? I'm stranded down here and I have to call someone in the States to come get me."

"Stranded huh? Have you eaten?"

"No, not really."

"Well, come on over here and let's get you fed first. Then you can make your call. Hell, even prisoners get to make a phone call. At least, they used to."

After eating, the *gringo* ushered Lupe into the office to make her phone call. It wasn't his phone, but he didn't see any harm in one phone call to the other side of the border. He gave her privacy by waiting outside. As she waited for the call to connect, Lupe looked through the office window and again saw the young woman wearing her red dress.

Outside Waltonville, Aztlán

Back at *La Casa Salamanca*, Eberto Aguirre was getting ready to go to the firehouse when the phone rang.

"Hello?"

A recorded message played on the line, "This is a

collect call from.... Guadalupe..... To accept the charges say yes"

"Yes"

"Eberto? Is that you?"

"Lupe, you're alive. Thank God."

"What the hell is going on, Eberto? Nestor is dead."

"Where are you? I'll send someone to pick you up."

"I don't have a passport or money or anything. How am I gonna get back?"

"Lupe, we're *coyotes*, remember? Where are you? "

"Tell them I'll be in the plaza across from *Iglesia de Santa Josephina.*"

"You just stay put. I'll have someone there in less than an hour"

"Eberto, tell them that I'm wearing a red dress."

Nuevo Laredo, Mexico

The *gringo* patiently waited outside in the donkey cart. He tried not to brighten up when Lupe emerged from the office, but she had that effect.

"So, did you get through?" said the gringo.

"Yes. Thank you so much for your help."

"Do you want me to stick around to make sure?"

Aztlanicon
Cast Unto This Veil Of Misery

"Oh no. That's fine. Thanks, you've already done so much."

He climbed back into the cart, took the reins and turned to her. "Look, if things don't work out, you're welcome to come out to the encampment. We've got room for you."

"Thanks, I'll do that if I have a problem. Where is it?"

"It's that way, a couple of miles north of town. More than a couple really. Ask anyone how to get to *La Cuadrilla Magica*. They won't take you there, but they'll know where it is."

The *gringo* compassionately urged the tired old donkey onward. Lupe watched as the cart pulled out onto the pavement and down the road. For a moment, she wasn't sure he was going to look back, but she was bolstered when he did. At least she wasn't completely undone.

Behind the large fountain in the church courtyard, Lupe could keep track of the plaza. It was a hectic gathering of stalled migrants and idle locals across the street. Boom-boxes sprayed music and advertising of clashy cultures and conqueror languages. The confluence of noise made for a tense, chaotic atmosphere as these denizens tread lightly through the faithless borderland, until that great day when enough cash has been gathered to pay for a *coyote*. Until then they peddle whatever it is that they have to sell.

Lupe watched the pretty local girl hold court in her red dress. She took comfort in knowing that she looked much better in it She hoped that the attentive young men were enjoying her perfume that surely lingered on the garment.

Suddenly, an old van stopped in Lupe's line of sight and she could no longer see the local girl. The driver jumped out brandishing an automatic weapon and ran around the van, out of sight. Shots rang out, so many you couldn't keep count. Lupe could see people spread out on the plaza. More shots fired. Lupe heard the van door slam shut. The driver ran back around, jumped in and drove away.

The local girl in the red dress was gone and all that remained were the bodies and blood of her dead admirers. Things were even worse than imagined. That fucker Eberto was in on this. How was she going to get home now? What are they going to do when they realize that they got the wrong person? She needed to hide. She grabbed her suitcase and hurried down the road. Maybe she could catch up. After all, that donkey was old.

Emotionally exhausted, Lupe sat on the side of the road. She could barely muster the will to lift her head off of her knees as the donkey cart seemed to come out of nowhere to stop right in front of her.

"Didn't work out?" said the *gringo*.

"It didn't work out." said Lupe. "I thought you were way up ahead of me?"

"Hop in. I want to get back to the encampment before dark. On a full moon like this the *djinn* will be around making mischief. I want to be safely by the bonfire at that point."

END OF VOLUME ONE

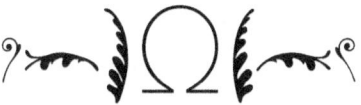

FOREIGN PHRASES FROM THE TEXT

Ándale-pues (Sp) = Alright then.

atmanjali mudra (Sk) = mudra *Virgen* on front cover is performing

La tierra promesa est aqui y ahora = The promised land is here and now.

la vida loca (Sp) = the crazy life

Poco Despues (Sp) = A little later

sangre azul (Sp) = blue blood, no moorish or jewish blood

Gringoñol
A PARTIAL SPANGLISH GLOSSARY

amenazar = to threaten
alambrista = illegal immigrant
alcachofa = artichoke
alocado = crazy person
alondra = lark
alquimia = alchemy
alquitrán = tar
alterer = to agitate, to fluster
asesinato = assassination
amasia = mistress
amarrete = mean, tight
amigote = pal
anciano = elder (tribe, church)
altura = height, depth, level, latitude
alucinación = hallucination
alucinante = hallucination
afliada = sharp
alianza = alliance

alzamiento = uprising, revolt
angélica = unmarried girl
amigoization = Mexicanization of Aztlan
aquejado[da]- de = suffering from
avocado = Uncle Tom [*ahuacatl* [Nahuatl]]
ayunas = without having eaten
Aztlán = imaginary land
Aztláno = one who inhabits this imaginary land

B

babiche = son of a bitch
babalawo = priest / witch doctor
barrio = neighborhood
bateria = legal term of battery
banco = bank, sperm donar
borderigena = border citizen
barracón = warehouse, slave quarters
bicha = vermin
bizco (ca) = cross-eyed
boquiabierto, ta = open-mouthed, astounded
bote = can, jar, boat
bozal = muzzle
bribón = scoundrel, rogue
brevedad = shortness

C

camarra = chamber
canochi (spang) = a Mexican living south of the Rio Grande.
canquiza (kan`KEE`za) = beating
caótico (ca) = chaotic
carnal = brother
carnalismo = brotherhood
casteyanqui = mestizo lanuage
casualidad = casualty
caudillo = chief of state
chale = ex. of disagreement. Also used for goddamit
chicas = girls
chihuahua = little Taco Bell dog
chusma = rabble, mob
ciénaga = bog , marsh
colmo = height [*para colmo de degracias* = to crown it all]
colonia = colony [*colonia proletaria* = shanty town]

colectividad = community

comercio = trade [*libre comercio* = free trade]

cometa = comet

cometido = mission, task   2. duty

comezón = itch, itching

conocimiento = consciousness

concepcion = conception

confidente = confidant

cincuenton, -ona = fifty year old   (*algo* = something)

clarividencia = farsightedness

comadreja = weasel

cretino = cretin

cuadrilla = gang

cubierto, ta = overcast

cuerva = female crow

cuesta = downhill

culto = cult

cumbre = summit

 D

de granja = free range

desafortunado -da = unfortunate, unlucky

despues = after (*despues de todo* = after all)

desquite = revenge

detonar = to detonate

delincuencia = crime; - *delincuencia juvenil* = juvenile delinquency

demencial = chaotic

defensa = defender

derota = unsuccessful person

Dios de Guadalupe = Day of Guadalupe

diario = diary

domina (LT) = master, mistress

E

eencina = California live oak

enemistad mortal = vendetta

energia = energy

enfermedad = disease

encubierto, -ta = covert; hidden

escondido = secluded [*a escondidas* = in secret]

esquina = corner

escoria = scum

escombros = rubble
escarnio = mockery
escalfar = to poach
escándalo = scandle
este = east

F

flecha = arrow
flotar = to float
fluvial = river
fluctuar = to fluctuate
florecer = to florish
foco = center, focal point
fofo = flabby
fogata = bonfire, fire
forajido = outlaw
foraneo = foreigner
forastero = stranger, outsider
forcejear = to struggle
forjarse = to carve out
flujo = flow (*flujo de caja* = cash flow)
flote = afloat (*salir a flote* = to get back on one's feet)
foco = center, focal point
frontera = border

G

gab acho = white guy, frog
grata ,- to = pleasant
gringófobo = a person who dislikes gringos
gringólatra = a persona who adores Gringo culture
gringoñol = mestizo language, part English, part Spanish
gruñón = grumpy
guadaña = scythe
güevón = bloody idiot
guacho,-cha = illegitimate child
guarango, -ga = coarse, vulgar
guarida = lair, hideout
guarro, -ra = filthy dirty pig
guión = screenplay, script
gusano = worm

H

hechecero (ra) = sorcerer, witch, wizard
helado = frozen over
hegemonia = dominance
herrumbre = rust
hermosa = beautiful
hermosura = beauty
heredera = heiress (*borracha heredera* = Intoxicated heiress)
heroina = heroin
hoja = blade
hondonada = hollow
hondura = depth
honestidad = honesty, modesty, decency; fairness
horgareño, ña = family
hoguera = bonfire [*morir en la* - = burned at the stake]
horroroso(sa) = horrid (idea, place)
horrendo (da) = horrific
huevos = eggs, testicles
huelga = strike
huelguista = striker
huevón = stupid bastard
humareda = cloud of smoke

I

imprudente = reckless (*temerario -ria*)
ingrato (ta) = ungrateful
inútil = useless (*niñoinútil* = useless boy)
inverso, sa = opposite, inverse
invidente = blind
invierno = winter
iracundo, da = angry, irate
izquierdo, da = left (*de izquierdas* = left wing)

izda = left (abbr.)

joder = to fuck [! *no jodas* ! = bollocks]
jornada = working day

L

lesbiana = lesbian
libre cambio = free trade
lucha = struggle
lucubrar = to rack one's brains over
ludopatia = pathological addiction to gambling
lujuria = lust
luto = mourning   [*de luto* = in mourning]

M

machista = male chauvinist
magico = magical
majadero (ra) = idiot
manitas = hands
manga = eat
maricón = queer (derogatory)
masificacion = overcrowding
matamoscas = flyswat
matanza = slaughter
mazorra = psychiatric hospital
mezcla = mixture; blend
mezclar = to mix; to blend
miramiento [andarse con ~s] = to stand on ceremony.
mecha = wick, fuse
miedo = fear [*tener miedo a* {or *de*} = to be afraid of ~]
miedoso -sa = fearful
miembro = member
migra = immigration police
Miraflores = Panama Canal locks near the Pacific end
mofa = mockery
M.O.F.A = Movimiento Oculto Florecer Aztlán.
muladhara = root chakra
muchedumbre = crowd, throng, great number, masses
mujere = woman
mujerzuela = loose woman
muy = very

N

nadie = nobody
necedad = stupidity, foolishness {*decir necedades* = to talk nonsense}
niños (ñas) = children
Noche Triste = Sad Night = the Aztecs failed to finish.off Cortez.

O

ocupacion = occupation
odio = hated
oeste = west
oferta = offer
orishas = the Gods of certain 'religions'

P

paja = straw [*hombrepaja* = strawman]
pasillo = corridor [*pasillo de muerto* = corridor of death]
parlanchín = chatterbox
partido = party
pendejo = fool, asshole
perro = dog
pésimo(ma) = lousy, poor quality (also *fatal*)
pinché = damned, kitchen boy
pochismo = ideology behind the *pocho* attitude toward life.
pocha (cho) = gringo-ized
pochista = person living between two worlds of Spanish and English.
prima = bonus
puertá = gateway, opening
punto muerto = deadlock
puto, (ta) = male prostiitue, whore

Q

querida -do = lover, darling
quietate = quiet, be still

R

rasquachismo = comfortably downtrodden; making the most from the least.
raza = race (la raza = the race)
realidad = reality

rebelión = rebellion
respiro = rest, breath

sabiduria = wisdom
sacapuntas = pencil sharpener
sabandija = worm
sabueso = bloodhound [*perro*] , sleuth [*policia*]
salsa = spice [*en su propria salsa* = in one's element]
salvador = savior
sanguijuela = leach
sanguineo = sanguine, self-confident
santero = Santeria priest, practitioner
sarcófago = meat-eater
secaucus = psychiatric hospital
segundo = second in command
sensitivo = sensitive
sherife = sheriff
significante = significant other
soberania = sovereignty
sobredosis = overdose
sobrenatural = supernatural
sobrenombre = nickname
sobrestimar = overestimate
sombre = shadow
sufrido(da) = longsuffering
suspecha = suspicion
sushumna(Sk) = central channel

temerario (-ria) = reckless (imprudente)
testigo = witness
telenovellas = TV stories, soap operas
tijereta = earwig
tribu = tribe
tuberius = water pipe

utopianista = one aligned with the pursuit of Utopia

vacuidad = emptyness
valiente = courageous
vanguardia = vanguard
venérea = venereal
vulgaridad = vulgarity
vuelco = upset

yegua = mare
yerbatero = healer
yermo, ma = barren
yacimiento = bed, deposit
yanqui = yankee
yonqui = junkie

zopenco, -ca = nitwit
zoquete = ankle sock; blockhead

(Sp) = spanish, *español*

(Sk) = sanskrit

Raw Preface of Sangs.gyes rDo.rje

Sangs.gyes rDo.rje. am what. fleshbound call, rin.po.che:
Sambhogakaya dimension. outreaches. to You.
Kali Yuga is immanent,

For the Godhead Which You Shall Never Fathom;
Current COSMIC CYCLE.has become tiresome.
Old Ways sufficient no longer.
GREAT SLEEP CYCLE.has begun:

MULATANTRA OF AZTLAN·
Guru Yoga.

ENVISION: TIGLE. primordial A inside of: radiates
WRATHFUL ELEMENT COLORS
Two DAKINIS:up-hold picture
GUADALUPE & SACRED HEART

With Eyes-open. be lightly focused on primordial A
Gradual REALIZATION. have that
DARK DAKINIS. hold MIRROR, not picture
MIRROR pointed. YOU. is
GUADALUPE & HEART SACRED. YOU. are
DWELL in that dimension.long as can

MONGREL-IGION TIME has begun.
MIXED BREEDS. stupid. much less
KALI YUGA TERMA. buried in YOU.
May the GREAT PERFECTION survive within
the reach of human consciousness.

NOTE: The <u>back cover</u> of this book is a manifestation of the telepathic
GURU YOGA and is for scrying at the hour of the full moon . The <u>front
cover</u> is for scrying at the hour of the new moon.

www.ingramcontent.com/pod-product-compliance
Lightning Source LLC
Chambersburg PA
CBHW020828260626
47169CB00003B/883